Call Me Lucky

Caroline Bell Foster

Editor: Alec Hawkes
Cover: Heidi Hargreaves - Dukki Design
www.dukkidesign.co.uk
Author's Photograph: Brian Bell
Published by: Sunshine Publications
www.carolinebellfoster/sunshinepublications
ISBN-13: 978-0993067310

Dedicated to...

The Original Night Team: Adam, Carol, Dawn, Dee, Gemma, Noreen, Paul, Rob, Sam, Tasha, Yvonne and Waseem.

PROLOGUE

It was always the same! They would laugh and joke around and then they would all turn on her. Felicity 'Fliss' Pecora hugged her head to her knees as she sat on the stairs. She always found solace on the quiet stairwell between the ninth and tenth floors.

The building was empty apart from the eighth floor which the night team occupied. No one came or went or even ventured on the floors above. It was only here where she could walk around in the darkness, be nobody, only a shadow. She liked that feeling of nothingness, of being able to creep about without anyone watching and no one to answer to, no one to report to and most of all no one to depend on. She depended on herself. If she let herself down only she was to blame and she liked it that way.

A silent drop of water trickled down her face and she dashed it away with an angry hand. It wasn't a tear! She never cried. Hell she had nothing to cry about!

Getting up she opened the double doors to the tenth floor. It was dark and shadowy, but she wasn't scared of the dark any more. At a young age she'd learnt that the darkness kept you hidden. Her mother couldn't scream at her if she couldn't see her. Darkness gave her peace and solace when chaos was all around her.

Walking around the pods and noseying at each one, Fliss trailed nail bitten fingers over photos of smiling partners and children. One even had a picture of a cute lop-eared rabbit.

This floor was a lot cleaner than her floor, she noticed. Probably because there were more floor captains and a couple of managers on this floor during the day.

The whole building was owned by QB. The Quintessentially

British company that sold 'Britishness' to foreigners. The cottage holidays catalogue around the British Isles was a big seller and so were the Keep Calm posters. QB sold anything that had a Union Jack on it. It was a fun job talking to wealthy Americans who loved talking to real 'English' people.

Fliss went stealthily into an office and for a moment caught her own reflection in the window. She was startled by how angry and hard she looked. Her dark blonde-brown curly hair was caught up in a tight, heavily gelled pony tail. Her eyebrows were dark, thin and straight. She hated her eyes as people always commented on them. They were a sort of brownish, bluish, greenish shade. Not hazel, not anything really. Just like her. A mixture of everything she hated. No history or culture. She checked herself as 'Other' on Government forms. Insignificant.

With a snort she sat on the wooden desk and pulled off her blue tracksuit jacket. It was hot and stuffy. The day team didn't give a toss about the night staff, she mused. How the hell did they expect them to work in this closed, stifling place? The air conditioning automatically turned on again at six, so by the time the day teams started to trickle in the building was nice and cool. Wankers!

Fliss dug into her pocket searching for the packet of painkillers she always kept. Then, going into the little fridge under the desk, she helped herself to a can of pop and swallowed the pills. The ache in her back would go in a moment she hoped.

With a wariness she strived to ignore she pushed a stack of papers off the desk—just because she could—and went down the stairs.

Della was right about one thing though this was her fourth job in a year and she needed to keep it. She had plans.

Fliss stopped at the vending machine to get a couple of chocolate bars before walking that long walk down to where the night teams always worked. There were about forty of them in each night working on what should be a four night rota. Most of them worked overtime.

Her team consisted of fun, lovable Della. She really clicked with her and was how she thought a mother should be. Della didn't look a day over thirty five, yet was older. She had long dreadlocks to her waist and always wore loads of chunky, brightly coloured costume jewellery.

Then there was Ingrid who, in her opinion, had the personality of cold wet fog. She had no time for Ingrid. She sat beside Priya. They'd actually gone to the same secondary school but they hadn't been friends back then.

Mackenzie sat opposite them and was gorgeous to look at, not that she liked burly blond men. But he was nice like Lucia the uni student from Spain. Jarrett was at the far end of the pod and was usually quietly reading a book or something between calls, but often came out with some brilliant one liners with his strong Nigerian accent that had everybody laughing. They were a good enough bunch to work with, especially as they all worked as many extra hours as they could get away with.

The pod was designed to work everyone to death with the minimum of contact with another human being as they were divided by high partitions that extended passed each desk. The only time they could speak to anyone was to stand up and then their headsets were so short they couldn't move around much.

The pod beside them had a radio, but theirs had been taken off them when Fliss had turned it up a bit too loud and Monica-Louise, their floor captain, had taken exception. The silly cow!

Jamming her headset on her head she took a deep breath and put on her posh voice to take a call.

"Thanks for calling…"

CHAPTER ONE

"I almost got my ears twisted off today." Mackenzie announced, standing up and placing an elbow on a partition on either side of him. It was early by their standards, after one o'clock in the morning and what they'd coined the American Rush hour was over until the next wave of calls in about an hour's time.

"Twisted off?" Lucia asked, confused, stretching her arms above her head and turning her head left to right and back again to ease the knot at the nape of her neck.

"All the swearing. I was talking to my nan today and had to stop myself turning the air blue with bad language. My nan has been known to twist my ears for much less." He explained affectionately then pointed across the pod. "It's her," he looked at Fliss who was on a call. "She's the bad influence."

Lucia chuckled. "I can't imagine Fliss stopping swearing, can you? It's as natural to her as breathing." Lucia gathered her long hair over her shoulder and started plaiting it.

Fliss, aware that they were talking about her, finished her call and stood up too. "What is natural to me?"

"Swearing and cussing people out." Lucia confirmed with a knowing smile. Winding Fliss up was one her favourite things to do. Fliss was so easy to rile. "Mackenzie says you're a bad influence."

"I don't even talk to you half the fu-bloody time Mackenzie, so I don't see what your problem is." Fliss crossed her arms over her chest and glared at him.

"Whoa there cowgirl." Mackenzie interrupted, quickly putting his arms up in surrender. Fliss was becoming more and more irritable these days he mused, anything would set her off. "I was simply suggesting that we all," he pointed to everyone, "start watching what we say. We swear too much."

"He means you," Lucia stressed.

"You do it the most Fliss," he admitted cautiously. "But I think we all need to stop. We've even got Jarrett using the 'F' word with a Nigerian accent."

Fliss shrugged.

"How about we place a bet?" Mackenzie asked them all.

"I don't bet," Fliss stated, checking her pockets for her lighter. "Well not with money."

"Anyone who says the 'F' word has to buy everyone a drink from the machine." Mackenzie went on as though she hadn't spoken.

"That's stupid and I'm not fu—" Fliss caught herself. "I'm not doing that."

"That's because you'd lose." Lucia laughed. "I may as well place my order with you now," she teased cheekily. "A hot chocolate please."

There was a chorus of 'I'm ins' from the rest of the team.

"Just you now Fliss." Lucia looked at her expectantly.

"Oh for goodness sake." Fliss sighed dramatically, putting a cigarette in her mouth. "Okay I'll do it."

"Every four letter word is out?" Ingrid asked.

"Starting when?" Jarrett asked, rolling back in his chair and standing up as he was seated at the far end of the pod and could only see the tops of their heads.

"How about now?" Lucia looked at Mackenzie for confirmation.

"I counter bet that Fliss will be the first to screw up." Ingrid put in quickly.

"Now hold on," Fliss swung round to Ingrid. "That's not-"

"Fail, Ingrid!" Lucia exclaimed. "You said s-c-r-e-w."

"That's not four letters." Jarrett said, stating the obvious.

Mackenzie slapped the partitions, winced and turned his hands over to see two angry red lines on them. "Just to clarify before you start arguing," he rubbed his hands together easing the pain. "Any word you wouldn't say in front of my nan. How's that?""

"We don't know your nan." Jarrett put in.

"Exactly. She's a lady but will happily twist off all your ears if you cuss in front of her." He winked, then looked at the time on his phone. "Bet starts now."

***

"Felicity, a word."

Fliss jumped, almost knocking over the cup of water that should not have been on her desk in the first place. She hadn't heard the floor captain approach and suspected she may have fallen asleep. It wasn't busy and it wasn't quiet either, it was an easy shift, but she just couldn't shake this tiredness. She needed to get herself some iron tablets.

"Coming. What should I put myself on?" She called out, not knowing which of the three digit codes to use to sign out of her phone. Everything they did had a code from a sale on a call, needing a few moments from a difficult call, to going to the bathroom. Everything they did was timed and logged into a database for someone somewhere to analyse. Not a single second was wasted on non-productivity. The company knew everything they did.

"Three zero seven."

Fliss tapped in the code which corresponded with the floor captain's monthly meeting, problem was, Fliss thought biting her lip, it was the middle of the month. Maybe she had fallen asleep, but then again, maybe not. The volume on her phone was set so high that people in the next building could hear if she got a call. She'd done something else wrong.

"Take a seat." Monica-Louise invited.

Fliss reluctantly took a seat to the side of the other woman instead of opposite. She really didn't want to see the smug look of satisfaction on her face whilst getting a verbal bollocking.

"Every quarter the company takes an interest in those employees who have done exceptionally well." Monica-Louise explained. "Targets met," she listed on her fingers. "No late or sick days, accolades from customers, amongst other things."

Fliss nodded, not knowing where this was going.

"This quarter we've chosen you."

Fliss stared at her blankly. Chosen her for what?

The floor captain smiled and leaned back in her chair pulling her extensions over one shoulder to finger comb them

"Me?" Fliss said, trying to remember the conversation.

"I know we don't particularly get on," Monica-Louise admitted with a shrug, flicking her hair back over her shoulder. "But you are a damn good sales agent and have given this team a much needed boost. You deserve to be recognised."

"I don't know what to say."

"There'll be an award for you, a write up on the company website, two hundred and fifty pounds for you to spend as you please. Four hundred pounds for the team to spend in London." Monica-Louise paused, smiled widely and held out her hand. "Congratulations and well done Felicity, you almost single handily won the team second prize for the Christmas bonus."

Fliss shook her hand and stood up. She'd never won anything in her life. "Thank you."

"Now don't start slacking," the floor captain warned. "I'll be keeping an eye on you."

"I won't."

"Oh and before you go,"

Fliss turned wearily back to her.

"I know we aren't friends Felicity but I have noticed you don't seem your usual self of late."

Fliss wrapped her arms around herself and tipped her chin up. "I'm fine."

"Everything okay at home?" Monica-Louise pressed.

"Yes."

"These shifts can wreak havoc on your health. Do you want me to book you in with the company doctor? It's a free service and confidential?"

"No, I'm fine. Everything's great." Fliss turned to go.

"Do you want to tell the team the good news or should I?"

"You can."

Monica-Louise looked at her with concern, nodded, then turned to her screens. "Get back on the phones," she ordered briskly, "We have eighteen calls waiting."

CHAPTER TWO

The calls were intermittent. When it was busy it was really busy with Monica-Louise calling out the amount of calls in the queue every thirty seconds, and then it would go really quiet as though someone in the world had flicked a switch. It was the most unpredictable shift Fliss had ever been on.

Feeling as though she was in the need of a nicotine fix, Fliss, making sure the floor captain wasn't around, pulled out her phone hidden between the pages of a catalogue and checked the time. She had another nine hours of this shift to go and another three hours before her next break. It was going to be a long night.

The beep signalling an incoming call sounded in her headset and she put on her posh voice.

"Thank you for calling QB, my name is Felicity. How may I help you?"

"Good evening. Very sorry to ring so late at night my dear," a needy female voice replied. "But I thought if I don't do this now I'll forget and your brochure says you're open twenty four hours?" The voice sounded apologetic.

Fliss had heard it all before and picked up her pencil to draw a cactus on her notepad. If only she could close her eyes instead of having to troll through various screens to take the order. It should have been a simple task but the software system they used was more flamboyant than practical.

"Yes we're here for your convenience." Fliss drew some spikes on her cactus tree. "May I take your name please?" She prompted again.

"Oh sorry dear,"

Fliss could hear shuffling.

"I've just lost the page."

Felicity gritted her teeth and started to shade in one of the three branches on her tree. "Not a problem, take your time." She pressed the pencil a little harder.

"Here it is. What did you ask dear?"

Fliss changed tactic. "Have you ever ordered with us before?"

"Oh yes. You have such pretty things. What would you like first?"

"Your name please."

"I've got a reference number," the lady went on. "Seven, two, eight, G for golf and F for Freddy."

Fliss switched screens, tabbed passed the name and address input page and entered the reference number, which in turn brought up all the customer's details.

"Thank you. Can you finally confirm your name and address please?" Fliss went back to her drawing and started shading in the other limb.

"Rossington." The lady faltered and Fliss heard an empty sigh. "I went back to my second husband's name as he was my favourite."

Felicity stopped drawing and smiled. She loved hearing these little titbits from customers and was always amazed at what people actually talked about. Della had once explained that for some old people this conversation was probably the only contact they had with another human being all day.

"I'm sorry dear, I'm eighty seven you know,"

Oh here we go, Fliss thought picking up her pencil, another old person thinking old age was a privilege which gave them a social standing above everyone else.

"Oh and I do forget things," she went on. "What else do you need?"

Giving up and knowing she'd probably be given a rollicking by that bitch Monica-Louise, Fliss decided to leave the script. There just wasn't any point sticking to it and old people could get very testy and rude sometimes.

"Take your time Mrs. Rossington," Fliss soothed, leaning back into her chair to admire her drawing. She'd never been good at art, but she could draw trees. "How can I help?"

"Bless you. What was your name again?"

Fliss sighed silently. "Felicity, Mrs. Rossington."

"Very pretty name Felicity, not common." Mrs. Rossington complimented. "My full name is Elizabeth April Rossington," she said briskly.

Oh what the hell, Fliss thought she may as well enjoy the conversation. "That's a lovely name Mrs. Rossington."

"My mother wanted to name me April but my father said no daughter of his was having a name like a prostitute!" She laughed and Fliss joined in.

"It's still very pretty Mrs. Rossington. What can I help you with today?"

"I need to send a present for my friend Izzy. She lives in New Orleans and is turning eighty five."

"Not a problem. What date?"

"The seventeenth my dear. She just loved being younger than me." There was another tinkle of laughter. "I want to send her something sassy, quintessentially British, but sassy. Izzy used to do my hair."

"Your hair Mrs. Rossington?" Fliss encouraged, looking at the time on the phone, four minutes in and she hadn't taken the order yet.

"That's right." Fliss could literally hear the smile in Mrs. Rossington's voice. "I used to sing and tap dance in a troupe. I danced right across Europe for all the soldiers, British, French and American. The Americans were the most fun though."

"Wow, I bet you have some stories to tell." Fliss was genuinely intrigued and wanted to know more.

"I sure do honey." Mrs. Rossington adopted an American accent. "I'll tell you something though Felicity, I've still got better legs than Izzy!"

They both laughed, but Fliss saw Monica-Louise turn and look at her so she ducked down in her seat.

"Aww, you are lovely Mrs. Rossington. I could talk to you all night." She really could, Fliss thought.

"Bless you dear. Age is an awful thing. It creeps up on you and knocks you to your knees, especially when you're not ready for it. Of course I can barely walk across the kitchen floor much less do a shuffle-ball-change nowadays."

For a moment Felicity didn't know what to say. I'm sorry sounded so inadequate, but she said it anyway.

"I've lived a full and selfish life my dear. Had the most amazing friends, husbands who adored me and been all over the world. Now it's just me on the estate. No family, not even a cat." Mrs. Rossington's voice petered out.

"Mrs. Rossington?" Fliss whispered worriedly after several long, empty seconds went by. "Are you there?"

"Oh yes dear, sorry." She sighed. "Sometimes I get overwhelmed with sadness. Most of my friends are busy tap dancing in the clouds now."

"I'm sorry Mrs. Rossington."

"Not your fault my dear. How old are you Felicity?"

It was a personal question and Fliss avoided personal questions from customers. She had never, in all her months working here, ever given out her surname, much less her age.

"I'm twenty. Well almost." She admitted, uncomfortably ducking down further into her seat as she spied the floor captain leave the work station in the centre of the room and walk towards their pod.

"Ah, you have your whole life ahead of you. If there's one thing an old lady can tell you it's this. Life is an apple, Felicity, you've got to take a bite. Take a bite without apology!" There was another tinkle of laughter.

"I will Mrs. Rossington," Fliss promised, picturing a younger Mrs. Rossington dancing with the soldiers. "I will."

"Now," Mrs. Rossington said briskly. "Enough of that talk, lets find something sexy for Izzy."

***

Finally on her break, Fliss closed the cubicle door behind her, slipped the lock into place and stealthily stepped up onto the toilet seat. Reaching up, she released the grimy window latch and, learning from past experience, gave the window a mighty shove.

Regaining her balance, and with a muttered curse, she pushed the window out as far as it would go and leaned out, feeling a gush of air against her face. She should have gone downstairs but either she was becoming very unfit or the stairs were becoming steeper, she thought. She probably should stop smoking, she mused honestly, but damn it to hell, she was allowed at least one vice!

It was getting colder, she realised, zipping her thin tracksuit jacket up to her chin and pulling up the hood before lighting the cigarette. The night was clear, the stars huge in the moonless sky and, against her better judgement, she ruined her peaceful mood by remembering her day with a shiver that had nothing to do with the weather.

She'd gone home to check on her mother and to lie down for a bit because she'd been really tired after going to the supermarket. For once it had been just the two of them and she'd taken a shower. Fliss had been under the spray of water washing her hair when she'd felt a finger scrape down the length of her spine.

Furiously dragging in the minty smoke, she inhaled deeply and felt a sledgehammer hit her chest, as she remembered another of her mother's 'guests' had stood naked beside the bath touching himself. It was 'Pitface'.

She hadn't screamed when he'd stepped into the bath, grinning behind her, his penis jutting out like the evil weapon it was. Nor did she scream when he slid his thin pale body against her back. She'd calmly soaped her hands, turned to face him just as he was about to position himself and stuck her soapy fingers in his eyes and pressed. Hard. He'd screamed. She'd punched him in the face, sending him toppling out of the bath and sprawling onto the cracked linoleum floor with a heavy thump.

She'd left him there, grabbed her towel and, with soap clinging to her skin and shampoo foam dripping into her eyes, she'd grabbed her clothes, noticing that the locks on her bedroom door lay broken on the floor, as she ran downstairs.

Fliss had told her mother what had happened and watched knowingly as her mother muttered a curse and buried herself deeper into the sofa.

Fliss had got dressed behind the old shed in the back garden and left without a backward glance. She'd need to buy new locks for the doors again.

The soap was now making her skin itch and her hair had dried to a flat dullness as though she'd washed it in mud. But at least she'd got away. When a similar incident had happened a few years ago, she'd called the police and it had become so complicated Fliss had said that she'd lied otherwise they would have locked up her mother and she would have spent her teenage years in foster care. Fliss had learnt to take care of herself.

But the shame always followed her. The memory of her mother having sex for money with her school friend Marty, and his brother Teddy thinking she'd had something to do with it had stained her life forever. Every time she looked at herself she remembered the ugly words Teddy had called her that night all those years ago.

She leant further over the window sill and dropped the cigarette butt, hoping her aim would be spot on and the smouldering nub would land on the bonnet of Monica-Louise's flashy car. It did and, checking her phone for the time, Fliss quickly lit another cigarette.

She had to move out completely she thought. She was tired of it, so tired her bones ached with the stress of it all. She couldn't go back to her mother's house. Strange men coming and going, thinking she was like her mother. When she'd talked to her mother about moving, the older woman had cried, begged and threatened to kill herself if Fliss left her. Fliss had no choice but to stay. She'd bought herself a dog for added protection and put more locks on her door.

The door opened and, from her vantage point Fliss watched Priya rush into the bathroom, turn on the taps and hold her wrists under the running water. She seemed distressed about something, Fliss thought silently as Priya splashed water onto her face and then dried it roughly with a cheap, coarse paper towel from the dispenser.

Most people assumed Priya was Asian because of her name and dark hair, but in fact her father was Turkish and her mother Greek.

"Hey Priya."

Priya whipped round, searching for her voice.

"I'm up here."

Priya's eyes rounded in shock when she finally caught sight of the top of Fliss's head. "What are you doing up there?"

"Having a fag."

"Monica-Louise was just asking for you."

Fliss shrugged, but dropped the half smoked cigarette the same way as the first before jumping down, leaving the window open as she opened the cubicle door to join Priya at the row of grotty sinks.

"Monica-Louise is a controlling bitch."

Priya grimaced as Fliss's plain speaking always made her uncomfortable but she ended up agreeing and, as they leaned against the sinks, they chatted about just how controlling their floor captain was.

The bathroom door flew open and both girls turned in surprise to see the floor captain standing with her hands on her wide hips, glaring at them.

"Are you aware that you have been off your phone for over twenty five minutes?" Monica-Louise directed at Fliss, coming into the room and sniffing the air like a bloodthirsty hound on its first hunt.

"Why is that window open?" Monica-Louise asked suspiciously. "Have you been smoking in here Felicity? Because if you have, it'll be your last night working in this building!" The floor captain promised with a relish in her tone.

"Fu—"

Priya cut in quickly, stepping in front of Fliss. "I opened the window because it smelt funny in here."

The floor captain looked them both up and down with narrowed eyes. "Get back to your desks both of you, but be warned Felicity

Pecora, you are on borrowed time."

The two girls climbed the stairs leaving the floor captain to close the window.

"Why did you cover for me?" Fliss asked, perplexed, no one ever came to her rescue. No one.

Priya, who was one step above her, turned and shrugged her shoulders. "You'd do the same for me." She said simply, before turning to climb the stairs.

CHAPTER THREE

"Call for you Fliss," Jarrett called out, disturbing her light sleep. She was trying to stay awake, especially as this was their first night and the rest of the team had that first shift talkativeness going on, especially about their trip to London at the weekend.

Her mother had been entertaining 'new' friends last night and when strange people were in the house, Fliss stayed awake to stop any drama that would undoubtedly unfold and spill out into the street.

Sometimes Fliss really did want to move out, but she couldn't. Her mother wouldn't be able to function without her, especially on those days when she could barely lift her head off the worn blue and gold sofa.

Fliss hated that old sofa. It had always been positioned in the same place, practically centre of the room close to the TV. The one time Fliss had pushed it to the wall her mother had screamed blue murder and threatened to throw her out of the house. Her mother never slept anywhere else, leaving her bedroom to whoever was staying with them.

She could go for days without washing if Fliss didn't bathe her herself. Then a few days later would swing the other way, getting all dolled up, becoming Miss Suzy Sunshine, making dinner, buying things and cleaning the house and then back to the sofa she would go, where she'd vegetate on a steady diet of TV, fizzy drinks and cigarettes for days on end until her next outburst of energy.

Fliss had wanted to buy a new sofa for her when she had started getting a regular income, bringing home a catalogue and showing her a lovely leather three seater that wouldn't take up so much space, but her mother had gone into hysterics, crying and screaming. Fliss had never brought it up again.

"Do you want me to transfer or not?" Jarrett yelled, jolting Fliss out of her sad thoughts.

"Do you know who it is?" She asked, flexing her fingers. They felt as though she'd been writing for days on end and they throbbed at the joints.

Jarrett shook his head and disappeared from her view, but she could hear him apologising to the customer for keeping them holding and then asking their name and putting them on hold again.

Jarrett looked at her. "It's a Mrs. Rossington," he said.

A call was just announced in her headset. "Can you ask for her number and I'll call her back please?"

"Sure thing." He saluted Fliss

Fliss was confident Jarrett wouldn't take over the call. Some teams were known for stealing customers just to get the sale but they respected each other on this pod.

Finishing her call, Fliss brought up Mrs. Rossington's details and changed the code in her phone to ensure the floor captain knew she was making an outside call.

"Why are you on an outside call Felicity?" Monica-Louise, still looking at her bank of screens, called across from the station to ask.

Talk about a barracuda, Fliss thought. Did the woman not do anything but look at her call activity log?

"Calling back a customer." Fliss only answered because she knew she had to.

"Why?"

Fliss gritted her teeth. She would love, just love, to tell Monica-Louise where to get off one of these days. She hated being accountable to anyone even if it was their job. Leave her alone and she would get on with it.

"I was on another call and she asked for me directly."

"Fine."

No apology, no nothing, Fliss thought in disgust. This job was becoming a real strain. Monica-Louise was always on her case even though she met every raising target the floor captain gave her but she had no choice but to stick with it. She had plans.

"Hello?" She said, when the call connected. "Mrs. Rossington, it's Felicity."

"Oh hello my dear. That was quick."

"It was a quick order. How are you?" Fliss asked.

She liked Mrs. Rossington. If they had a reality show where customer service agents could meet with their customers Fliss would want to meet Mrs. Rossington face to face. She was lovely.

"It's coming up to Christmas and I always get into the spirit of things Felicity," Mrs. Rossington explained. "Giving a little here and a little there is how good Christians live," she advised with a tinkle of laughter.

"I understand Mrs. Rossington," Fliss answered. She had never had the luxury to spend whenever or however, but she always gave to the Salvation Army man who stood outside the supermarket ringing his bell every Christmas.

"Do you earn commission Felicity?" Mrs. Rossington asked. "I meant to ask you on my last order, but you know this old brain of mine forgets everything."

"I do Mrs. Rossington, but you can place an order with any of my colleagues," she replied, knowing every call was recorded and that was what QB expected her to say.

"No I only want you."

Fliss punched the air and grinned. Ingrid had a regular customer in America who placed huge orders with her all the time.

"Thank you Mrs. Rossington."

"Now tell me about that china set on page sixty seven of catalogue eight. Do you like it? I'm not sure about the pattern, is it too old fashioned?"

Fliss laughed. "I'll take a look but because of the whole data protection thing can you please confirm your address for me?"

They became friends, with the older woman telling Fliss lovely anecdotes that made her laugh and gave her advice about life, reminding her to take a bite of that apple. Fliss told her she would get a T-shirt printed with the slogan on.

Fliss always felt empowered and confident after speaking to Mrs. Rossington and she even fought the urge to look her address up online-which they all did-preferring to let her imagination run wild and respect her privacy.

Between her friendship with Mrs. Rossington and Della, Fliss was beginning to think she really could better herself.

***

It was a sweet little pub, untouched by the glass, dizzying strobe lighting and chrome of many of the other bars they'd been to that night. Priya and Mackenzie had gone off to the bar leaving Fliss to find a place for them to sit, which wasn't hard as there was a choice of three plush semi-circular couches third row in from the stage.

It was a strange little place, but Fliss liked its quirkiness, dark wood panelling scarred by age and memories. Tables lit by low brass lamps with patchwork glass shades and short metal chains. It was a place for lovers and secret lovers. A place to snuggle, to relax and to forget.

Fliss curled into one corner of a leather couch and hugged a velvety cushion, as she watched a tall thin man with brown hair get on stage and start to sing his own rendition of *Crazy for You* in a low, deep, soothing voice. He must have started the evening wearing a suit Fliss mused, noticing the absence of his jacket and tie. His shoes were polished to a high sheen, his shirt undone at the throat and a black cummerbund hung low on his hips. He looked familiar, but she didn't know anyone in London.

There was a sign behind him that said 'Open Mic Every Night.'

"Nice place this," Mackenzie said, sliding down beside her and fluffing a cushion for Priya as she sat on his other side.

"We are staying here aren't we?" Priya asked with a tinge of exasperation. She didn't really understand the need to go from bar to bar all night long and when she'd complained they'd laughingly explained this was something of a British tradition, the pub crawl. It was already after two in the morning and she'd lost count of all the bars they'd been to.

Within a week of taking second place, Mackenzie had badgered management enough to let them take their prize in December. They'd all travelled down by train that morning and she was tired.

Priya turned to look at Fliss, who was humming to the song with a dreamy expression on her face.

"Go up and sing," Priya encouraged.

Fliss looked at her in horror and shook her head so violently the gold hoop earrings she wore bounced against her neck. "I can't do that."

"You can sing Fliss?" Mackenzie asked, whilst flicking through his messages on his phone.

"No."

"Yes she can.," Priya answered Mackenzie, cutting off the other girl. "Her mum told me she should audition for that talent show on TV, she's that good."

"As my mother is normally out of it I wouldn't read too much into what she says Priya." Fliss dismissed tightly.

The man on stage was now singing an old 50's song she didn't recognise so, ignoring her friends, allowed herself to be transported to a place of softness, light and dreams.

"I bet you twenty quid to get up there and sing Fliss," Mackenzie challenged sometime later with a smirk.

"Don't be such an ass Mac." Fliss told him, moving forward to pour herself a glass of water from the jug a waitress had helpfully placed on their table. God knows she wasn't a drinker, but the one little shot she'd had to try simply because it glowed in the dark had gone straight to her head and she was feeling a little reckless. Reckless, but not stupid she corrected silently and changed the subject by asking, "I wonder how the other lot are doing?"

Mackenzie reached for his phone he'd chucked down onto the table sometime ago and scrolled rapidly through his text messages.

"Lucia texted that they're all back at the hotel. That was about an hour ago." He carelessly put his phone down again and, leaning back, decided to have a little fun. "Fifty quid Fliss."

Fliss ignored him.

"Seventy."

"Will you stop!"

"Look at it this way, Fliss," Mackenzie went on. "We're in London, on an all expenses paid trip and you don't know anyone. You've got nothing to lose," He encouraged. He could see she was wavering. "All right a hundred quid." He enticed, fishing into his pockets and pulling out a bunch of crumpled twenties, straitening and counting them out before slamming them down on the table in front of her. "I dare ya," He challenged, cocking a blond brow at her.

It was a long way to the stage, no one was watching, everyone was talking and laughing and she could hear the chink on chink sound of glasses being washed at the bar. Then, closing her eyes she took a deep breath, leaned into the mic and sang.

"Can't hear ya love!" Someone shouted. "Turn on the mic!" There was a chuckle from the audience.

Snapping her eyes open and feeling the heat of embarrassment creep up her neck, Fliss felt along the smooth metal for the tiny switch she knew must be there but could not find it. Don't panic, she chanted to herself, don't panic. I can do this.

The same brown haired man, came up on stage, switched on the mic for her and gave her an encouraging smile before leaving her once again. I can do this, Fliss thought. She'd done these a thousand times before. Picture another place, be another person. You're wearing that red sequinned dress, the one with the split to the thigh. You're ten pounds lighter. You're five inches taller. You're wearing heels. You can do this.

The words flowed as she sang Amy Winehouse's *You Know I'm no Good*, and imagined herself at an exclusive charity event hosted by the young royals.

She finished with a flourish and a smile and opened her eyes. She'd done it!

The crowd was watching her in silence.

Oh God. Oh my fucking God! She thought.

With a sob, she clapped her hands over her mouth and ran.

CHAPTER FOUR

She ran passed the strapping black bouncer at the entrance, around the side of the building and passed a bunch of wheelie bins before stopping and throwing up against the building. Oh God it was horrible. They didn't like her. Her body crumpled against the wall and she pressed her forehead into it, feeling the rough brick bite into her skin. Any pain was better than the feeling of her dreams shattering.

"Fliss!" It was Mackenzie. She didn't want to talk to him. Not like this, not when she had failed. It was his fault anyway. She would never have put herself through this if he hadn't dared her.

"Fliss!"

"I'm here," She called out quickly, wiping away the water from her eyes. They were not tears she told herself.

"Why did you run you nit?" He admonished softly, pulling her into his arms and hugging her tight. "They loved you."

"Yeah right," she said pulling free and sniffing loudly. "Loved me enough they couldn't bring themselves to even clap Mac."

"They didn't get a—" he didn't finish what he was about to say as a man in dark jeans, white shirt and dark leather jacket walked towards them.

"If I didn't see it with my own eyes I'd have never believed chavvy Felicity Pecora could render my customers speechless."

Fliss gaped into the darkness knowing that voice, but refusing to believe it.

"What? Got nothing to say? This is a first," he chuckled and, stepping closer, held out his hand to Mackenzie. "Theodore Nicholson. But everyone calls me Teddy," he explained. "Felicity and I grew up together."

Mackenzie shook his hand. "Mackenzie. Nice to meet you. Are you coming back in Fliss? They want more."

Fliss shook her head in horror. There was no way she was going back inside. She'd done what she said she would do, gave it a go and took a bite of her apple. They didn't like her and she wasn't about to make the same mistake again.

"Can you give us a minute Mackenzie?" Teddy asked.

"Yeah, course mate." Mackenzie stepped away. "You were amazing Fliss. See ya in a bit."

Could this night get any worse. Teddy Nicholson was stood right in front of her, once again, at the lowest point of her life. World open up and suck me right in, she begged silently.

"Well?"

He'd used that same word with that same menacing tone that night all those years ago, she remembered with shame.

"Well what?" She questioned defensively, stalling.

"Well what are you doing in my pub for one thing?" Teddy asked, leaning against the wall and fishing into his jacket pocket for the one cigarette he allowed himself each week. It wasn't there.

She turned to look at him but he was in profile and she could barely see him in the darkness. "I'm in London," she mumbled.

"I noticed."

She was fifteen again. Spotty, ugly and fat. Reduced to the bumbling teenager who'd been crying in the jitty at the back of the house as he'd shouted at her mother for having sex with his brother Marty. He'd threatened to call the police and social services on them. He'd been so angry and had left through the back gate, finding her huddled against the fence.

He'd reduced her to even more tears by the time he'd finished with her and when she'd just about crumbled at his feet, he'd taken a huge breath, shoved his hands through his hair and then given her a long pep talk that basically said, if he could get out then so could she.

"We won a trip," she admitted quietly. "From work."

He moved then, turning to stand in front of her, his head cocked to one side as he looked her over. He looked at her feet in sparkly ballet shoes, her legs in dark skinny jeans and a sparkly silvery top with tiny straps over her shoulders. Her hair was in a tight bun, set high on top of her head. It looked like she had a silky doughnut on her head.

"You look really nice Felicity."

"What?" She snapped defensively, folding her arms over her chest. "You thought I'd still be wearing my charity labels Teddy?"

He frowned down at her. He'd always felt guilty for laying into her the way he had done that night behind her house. She couldn't help the way her mother was or the environment she lived in. He'd just been so mad that her mother had got money out of his baby brother for sex. Stealing his innocence.

"Maybe," Teddy shrugged. "Why deny it?"

Her eyes flashed and she poked him in the chest. "I'm not a kid any more Teddy." She lifted her chin and stared straight at him.

"Really?" He sounded sceptical. "You've changed?" He was remembering the scrawny kid with the foul mouth.

She took a shuddering breath knowing he didn't really believe her. Not that she cared what he thought.

"Yes really," she snapped. "Look, can you go and get my friends please. I'm not going back in there," she admitted tightly.

"You were sensational Felicity." He smiled down at her. "My crowd loved you."

"Yeah right," she scoffed. "They loved me so much my ears are still ringing from all the appreciation they showed!" She finished on a wobble. She was not going to get emotional, especially in front of him! "And why do you keep saying your crowd?"

"I own the place," he admitted. "And they were struck dumb by how good you sounded and not expecting it. Jesus Christ Fliss! Where does that voice come from? It's amazing."

"Stop lying Teddy."

"I'm not lying. They want more!" He grabbed her hand. "Come on let's go."

28

"Are you fucking crazy?" She yanked violently out of his grasp and stepped away from him. It was beginning to drizzle. It had drizzled that infamous night too.

He grinned at her. "Ah, now, here is the Felicity I know," he laughed. "I could always depend on your, dare I say, vocabulary to lower the tone of any conversation."

"You can say what the fu-hell you like." Why was she letting herself down like this, she thought, fighting the tears. "Please Teddy, go and get my friends. I'm getting wet."

"Only if you promise to come back tomorrow night and do a whole set. When are you going back up to Notts?"

"We've got another night," she said without thinking. "And I'm never going on stage again."

"Come back tomorrow and have dinner with me then."

"No. Why? So you can laugh at me. No thanks," she questioned and answered all at once.

He chuckled deep in his throat. "I want to know what's been going on with you, I'm curious that's all."

"You can take you're curiosity and sh—"

"How old are you?" He cut in and watched with amusement as a shade of red touched her cheeks. She'd always been fiery. She'd always fascinated him.

Fliss felt like an idiot. She didn't know why she was behaving like this in front of him.

"Twenty."

"Hmm. Come, I'll buy you a drink before you go." He took her hand.

"I don't drink." She grumbled.

He stopped walking and turned to look at her in that intent way of his, with his head to one side. He nodded silently and then did what he'd done all those years ago. With one hand he cupped her face and used his thumb to stroke her cheek. A tender moment from him. He shook his head as though getting rid of unwanted thoughts and dragged her inside.

***

The bar erupted into applause when they entered, with cheers and clapping from everyone.

"See Felicity," Teddy said grinning. "They loved you."

Fliss didn't know what to do or what to say, but clung to his hand as though her life depended on it.

"Another song?" He asked in a whisper only she could hear.

She shook her head. She couldn't, it was too much.

Understanding, he said something to the bartender, who grinned at her and poured her a glass of milk.

"Milk Teddy?" She asked when the noise had died down.

He grinned and in this light she could see the changes in him. His forehead had a few lines on it and a beard was threatening. His dark hair was combed out of his face, where years ago, it had flopped into his eyes. Ah, those eyes were still the same she noted, still very blue, but sparkling down at her now, instead of shredding her to pieces like before. He'd also grown into his ears she noted with a silent smile. How old was he now? Twenty-five? Twenty-six? He looked nice.

"You said you don't drink."

"I've not had milk since I was about six," she stated, somewhat sardonically, as Priya and Mackenzie joined them.

"Will you all come back tomorrow night? As my guests?" Teddy asked them after the introductions were made.

"It's not just us," Mackenzie revealed. "There's another load back at the hotel."

"Not a problem. See you at nine," Teddy confirmed.

"Sounds good." Mackenzie shook his hand, Priya waved goodbye and as Fliss turned to go Teddy caught her hand to stop her.

"You were amazing tonight Felicity Pecora," he stated softly, pulling her into his chest. "And I'm glad you got out."

She hugged him back wanting to tell him the truth.

CHAPTER FIVE

Fliss stood just inside the doorway of Teddy's pub letting Mackenzie introduce the rest of pod eight to him and his staff.

She didn't want to be here, had trailed around all the touristy bits of London with a sense of dread for this very moment.

Teddy knew her. He looked at her and probably remembered the mattress in her front garden, or that time her mother had a fight with the man at the corner shop, or even worse the time her mother slapped his mother right there on the street and the police had been called. Teddy knew too much about her.

"Coming in?" The man of her thoughts stood in front of her, minus the leather jacket of last night and wearing dark jeans and a dark shirt with the sleeves rolled up to his forearms. He looked different, intimidating in his masculinity and she'd never been more aware of a man.

She didn't want to be here and he must have seen something in her eyes as his mouth pulled down on one side and he looked at her, his blue eyes smouldering with an intent she couldn't decipher.

Fliss wanted to fold her coat around her some more, but that would look stupid so she tipped her chin up, daring him to say something. But without a word he took her hand and pulled her into the room.

It turned out to be a good night. Teddy had sat across from Fliss talking and laughing with the team as though he'd known them all his life. Then he'd hosted the weekly quiz night in which they, the 'Out of Towners', had won. The only one surprised Fliss had answered the majority of the questions had been Teddy.

Fliss watched in nervous amusement as Teddy promised her

team—mates that he would have her back at the hotel in time for their trip home tomorrow. Then he turned off the lights, leaving just the dim glow of down-lighters over the bar. He locked the door, leant against it and looked at her.

He'd always had feelings for Felicity, he acknowledged to himself. She'd been the thorn in his side for too many years, leading his little brothers into more trouble than he could count. An odd scrap of a thing with the blonde pigtails, brown skin and filthy mouth. Then she'd blossomed. A product of her circumstances but beautiful in that flaming, defiant way she had. Now, she was still a pain, only more of a pleasurable pain. He wanted her.

"Here." Teddy held out a glass to her.

"Milk? Again?" She smirked but accepted the glass. "I'm not a kid any more Teddy," she pointed out.

"I can't help myself. I've known you most of my life. I have memories of a snotty nosed kid knocking at my door asking if Timmy and Callum could come out and play at nine o'clock at night!"

"It was still light!" Fliss argued. She used to stay out as late as possible, anything but go home.

"It was too late for little girls to be playing out."

"I wasn't little," she grumbled, putting the glass down and folding her arms over her chest.

"But it was safer outside than in wasn't it Felicity?" He said softly reaching forward and peeling her arms apart. He entwined his fingers around hers.

He knew, Fliss felt that familiar ball of lead in the pit of her stomach and tried to pull her fingers free but he held on, forcing her to look at him. He lived on a different street but everyone in their neighbourhood knew of her mother. She was notorious for being loud and abusive and if you looked at her too hard, you'd be sure to get an earful.

"I'm glad you got away from it all Felicity," Teddy said, gently turning their hands over.

Fliss dipped her head, she was afraid. The only person who knew anything about her was Della and what she knew wasn't much. Fliss didn't do cosy chats with girlfriends where she revealed all about her home life. Hell, she'd never done cosy in any way shape or form and she didn't have any girlfriends.

"I still live there," she revealed quietly.

"What!" He let go of her hand. "Why?"

"She's my mother."

"She never looked after you!" He yelled, with eyes blazing at her in disbelief. "She allowed her druggie friends to shoot up in front of you!"

Fliss felt a tickling feeling behind her eyes. She was not going to cry. She didn't do tears!

"Yes but she loves—"

"Don't you dare," he roared. "Don't you dare defend her!" Teddy stood up to glare down at her. "She'd sell you to the highest bidder!"

Fliss flicked away a trickle of water from her cheek.

"I could have been fostered out, but she kept me," she begged him to understand. "She loves me."

"I should have protected you," he said grimly, walking over to the bar to pour himself a shot of whisky, gulping it down quickly, before turning back to her.

"I was not your responsibility."

"Your mother wasn't fit to look after you."

"She did the best she could," she defended. "I-"

"Do you know why I laid into you so strongly that night behind your house?" He interrupted.

Fliss shook her head. Whoever said knives hurt. His words alone had slaughtered her and still did whenever she could bring herself to remember them.

"I wanted you to take my words and do better for yourself," he admitted. "I wanted to cross paths with you years from that moment and hear you proudly telling me that I'd been wrong. That you had made it out! I wanted you to be anywhere but in that blasted neighbourhood, living in that house with a mother who didn't care about you!"

"As I said," Fliss seethed. "I am not, nor ever have been, your fucking responsibility!" She yelled, feeling a tide of fury take hold. "If I wanted help I could have got it. Do you think social services had never come knocking?" She prompted, not waiting for him to answer. "I made sure the house was clean and my mother sober enough to get rid of them! I never once went to bed hungry! How dare you think you know what's best for me!"

"I didn't mean it like it sounded—"

"Oh well that's okay then," she said sarcastically, her eyes cutting after him. "I can take care of myself. I'm working, I'm doing great." She grabbed her handbag and coat from the chair opposite. "So what if I live at my mother's house? It saves me a fortune on rent and I can make sure she's all right."

She stormed to the door, her back rigid with disappointment. She was doing all right by herself. Her life could have been worse.

"Let me out," She demanded, rattling the heavy door handle. She could feel him right behind her.

"I'm sorry," Teddy apologised just behind her. "I wasn't belittling you."

His hands were now on either side of her and Fliss leaned her head against the wooden door, refusing to acknowledge him.

"I'm sorry," he said again in her ear, his breath a hot whisper against her neck.

She felt exposed, wishing her hair were loose instead of up in its usual tight bun.

Fliss felt his hands on her bare skin, smoothing up and down from shoulder to elbow and back again. Her coat was folded over her arms and she held her bag tightly by its fancy metal strap.

"Do you want to know what else I dreamt about?" He asked.

Fliss shook her head. She didn't want to know and she didn't like feeling that pulse of awareness that refused to be ignored either.

"We're older, and me not recognising this beautiful woman in front of me," his hands stayed at her elbows drawing circles with his thumbs. "Like last night," he rubbed his temple against the side of her face, breathing in her scent. "For a moment," he admitted, sucking gently on her earlobe. "She has the body of my dreams. Large beautiful breasts and soft curves. Her skin is glowing and her eyes, oh God her eyes, still filled with fire, but passionate fire." He moved his hands to her shoulders. "If I turn you around now will I see that same fire?"

Heat shot through Fliss, scorching a path down her body to pool at that place between her thighs. There was a clink on the tiled floor where she'd dropped her bag. Her coat followed.

Teddy turned her to face him, his large hands moving to cup her face, his fingers beating an erotic drum at her nape.

"See," he said smugly, watching her closely. "She didn't disappoint. Fire in her eyes." He dipped his head and kissed her.

Fliss had been kissed before, but not like this. This was a demand. A demand to give herself wholly to him. He wasn't accepting anything less. She should have been afraid waiting for that moment when her mind shut down and she started methodically counting all the bricks surrounding her, protecting her. But this was Teddy, he would never hurt her.

Fliss opened her mouth letting him in and Teddy sank into her body, shifting his arms to cup her bum and drag her into him. The kiss deepened and one of them, Fliss didn't know who, made a sound deep in their throat.

Teddy walked her over to the bar, lifting her easily onto the polished surface, all the while sealing his lips over hers as his tongue played havoc, stroking, coaxing and teasing her mouth.

Fliss was lost, she'd never felt like this before. She'd read about it countless times, wondering if this feeling ever existed. Teddy gave her this feeling and she never wanted it to end.

A coolness touched her chest. Teddy had pushed her top up and was massaging her breasts through her bra. His fingers pinching her nipples as he ran his tongue down her neck.

Fliss's hand sought his hair so she could hold on to him. It was softer than it looked and he growled when she pulled it, pulling his mouth back up to hers.

Shifting again, Teddy pulled her bra down and sighed in pleasure at the sight of her brown nipples, large and inviting like taunting headlights on her body. He had never seen a sight so beautiful and closed his mouth around an erect nipple, sucking it deep into his mouth, grazing his teeth over it. Anchoring an arm around her waist, Teddy pulled her off the counter with urgent clumsiness.

Fliss felt her legs hit the back of a sofa but she didn't have time to register where she was, she just wanted, no needed to feel his skin. She pulled his shirt free from his jeans, gasping in pleasure as her hands moved under his shirt to feel the taut, hot skin of his back.

A tug here, a tug there and he had her jeans open, moving his hand inside to caresses her sex. Her panties were already damp and she whimpered in her throat as he shifted, taking her jeans and panties down as he knelt and breathed in her essence.

She smelt like ambrosia and sunny days. She smelt like tomorrow and promises. She was his.

Fliss had never felt like this before, she should be scared, she should be fighting him off but it felt right. This was Teddy. He knew her history and it didn't matter. Fliss let the tears fall as it was all so magical and for the first time in her life she allowed herself to let go and feel.

Teddy felt her tremors and gathered her close, his mouth seeking, finding and sucking the tiny nub within her folds. She pulled at his shoulders, his hair, conflicting fingers as she tried to push him off, yet demanding he stay.

Blowing against her heat and with a single rough swipe of his tongue she screamed, her knees giving way as he lapped and lapped and drank from her.

***

"I knew you would match my passion." Teddy revealed smugly a few moments later. They were sitting on one of the sofas, Fliss in her bra and jeans and Teddy shirtless.

Fliss didn't know what to say. Her one proper boyfriend last year had never done that to her. "Oh," she said lamely.

He chuckled and grabbed her around the waist to bungle her into his side, kissing the top of her head. "I didn't finish."

"Do you want me to…" Fliss started to suggest, heat gathering in her cheeks, as she saw the heavy evidence of his arousal behind the zipper of his jeans.

He laughed, shaking his head. He looked so happy Fliss thought, his blue eyes shining bright as he looked at her and then, frowning, he tipped her head down. He did a lot of that Fliss thought indulgently, turning her this way and that to his liking as though she were a doll.

"My dream," he clarified. "I didn't finish telling you about my dream. I had visions of you ranting at me with your hair loose too," he admitted. "Take it down for me."

It wasn't a request, she noticed and wanting to please him, reached up to pull the hairpins from her bun. She'd used a lot of pins.

"You're doing that on purpose," he growled a moment later as he watched the rise of her breasts, almost spilling out of her cotton bra whenever she lifted her arms to pull out a pin.

"Doing what?" She asked, looking over her shoulder at him.

Teddy was aware she probably didn't even know she was a born seductress. Looking at him now, her eyes tantalisingly dark green or brown, he couldn't tell which. Felicity's eyes were a mixture of her heritage, just like her hair. Light brown loose curls with streaks of gold. As a kid those golden streaks had been almost white. She'd always been unusually beautiful.

Hair finally down, Teddy gathered the silky tresses in his hands as it fell in waves to her shoulders. The front was stiff from all the gels she must have used in it and he smiled sitting behind her, his thighs on either side of hers. There was no one like her, he thought indulgently, as he began to pull the sticky strands apart.

Fliss had never in all her life felt so beautiful. Her hair was an inconvenience she never thought about. She washed it, she put it up. She never wore it down. But it was almost reverential the way Teddy was finger combing it and she moaned in pleasure.

"You like that huh?" He asked, massaging her head. He didn't wait for an answer. "You'll like this even more," he promised, trailing fingers down her spine to unclasp her bra, pulling it down her arms and dropping it beside her. He shifted again, cupping her breasts in his hands. She overflowed against his palms and Teddy massaged them, getting to know their weight and every curve, feeling her smoothness and what made her moan. He swept his fingers over her nipples again and again back and forth, sometimes hard, other times with a flicker as light as a butterfly's wing.

She was pressing into him, her head rolling back onto his shoulder and with deft movements he opened her jeans, pushed them down and used his fingers one, then two, to sweep inside her. She came apart in his arms and he loved it. She was his.

CHAPTER SIX

Locking the door behind them, Teddy turned to Felicity and planted yet another kiss on her already swollen lips. He just couldn't get enough of her, he thought, tenderly taking her hand to guide her up the shallow steps from his pub to the pavement.

"Do you see the twins often?" Fliss asked, with a tinge of sadness. The twins, Timmy and Callum, had been her friends. She remembered buying a ten pence mix of sweets for them all to share and going round to their house. Teddy's mum had answered the door and told her they weren't allowed to play with her any more. Fliss still remembered walking home fighting the tears and dropping the sweets one by one down the drain. Flying saucers, blue gob-stoppers and their favourite, white chocolate mice. She'd been about seven or eight.

"They're both in uni now, Timothy—we're not allowed to call him Timmy," he advised with a rueful smile. "Is up in Newcastle and Callum is in Brighton."

"They couldn't be any further apart," Fliss stated, sweeping the sad memories of her childhood to the back of her mind.

"They had a bit of a falling out," Teddy volunteered. "Over a girl of course." He finished bitterly.

"That's sad. They used to be so close."

"Yeah."

"What about your other brothers?"

Teddy came from a large family. He was one of seven boys spread between four different fathers. Teddy was the second eldest.

"Pauly, you saw yesterday," Teddy explained.

"When?"

"When you were singing, he was wearing the tux," he reminded. "Helped with your mic?"

"That was Pauly?" Fliss stopped and turned to him, remembering the man with the wonky cummerbund and gentle smile. She remembered thinking he looked familiar.

"Yeah." Teddy's smile turned sappy. "He owns a renovation company down here," Teddy told her with pride. "And trains kids in long distance running. He's in Europe for weeks on end."

"You're close?"

Teddy smiled. "Yeah."

"and the others?"

"Remember Marty?"

Fliss nodded. Marty had always been a bit wild.

"He's in prison," Teddy told her. "He stole one too many cars, and the last two kids are still at home.

They walked passed a sheltered bus stop advertising a new perfume. The large hands of a blue eyed model covered the breasts of a dark skinned girl. Teddy saw it as a sign. A very good sign.

"Do you go home often?" Fliss asked, interrupting his thoughts as they walked.

"Not really," he revealed. "There's nothing up there for me." He pulled her to a stop again and brought her hand to his lips. "But I'm sure I'll be going up there a lot more from now on." He tacked on watching intently and liking that her eyes turned a soft, pale, mellowy gold.

Fliss had thought it unnerving the way he looked at her. It was such a direct, penetrating blue gaze seeing too much, but she was getting used to it, even welcomed it. She didn't need to hide anything from him as Teddy already knew the horrid bits of her life story and was still holding her hand. She wanted to run out into the middle of the street with her arms open wide and sing to the stars.

"If you could choose a number between three and ten what would you choose?" Teddy asked, casually noticing that a light drizzle had started so scooped off his beanie and tugged it over Felicity's soft loose curls.

"Ten," Fliss answered without hesitation, adjusting his hat on her head. "Why?"

Amusement glimmered in his blue eyes. "No reason." But nodding to himself he smiled, his whole body relaxing, and again he kissed her, tucked her arm into the crook of his elbow and walked on. They hadn't walked very far, he noticed.

"Hungry?" He asked as they strolled passed a chip shop, a curry house and a fried chicken shop all in a row. The air was filled with the intoxicating aroma of mushy peas, exotic spices and cooking oil. A smell depicting modern day Britain.

"No, but you go ahead and order something."

"A kebab?" He encouraged. "A curry?" Teddy wriggled his eyebrows comically.

She wrinkled her nose. "Not at this time of night, no thanks." She had never been the type to go out get drunk and then binge on food before going home.

"I'll just get some chips."

Teddy was obviously a regular as the Asian lady behind the counter greeted him by name and asked if he was feeling all right when he didn't order his usual pie and chips with curry sauce on the side.

Lots of teasing and an open bag of chips, liberally doused in vinegar, later they left crossing a major intersection and eating the chips with tiny plastic forks.

Teddy turned them down a narrow leafy street and stopped in front of a three story Georgian house.

"I live on the top floor," he pointed out scrunching up the white, oil stained paper into a tight ball.

Fliss looked at the building bathed in the pale white light of a street lamp and mapped the windows on the third floor, that was his.

"If you go in there with me now," Teddy cupped her face tenderly and leaned his forehead against hers. "You know what will happen?" He warned, rubbing his nose against hers.

Fliss's body had been on high alert all evening, he'd given her relief, but not wholly. She wanted to share herself completely. This

41

was taking a bite of her apple. This felt right. This was Teddy. Creeping an arm up and around his neck she pulled him down and kissed him.

The smile he gave her when she released him made her toes curl and, taking her hand again, Teddy pulled her into the house, rushed her up the stairs and into his flat.

***

"What are you doing?" Teddy asked, coming up behind Fliss in the semi dark kitchen and watching in amusement as she jumped in fright. The only light came from a lamp in the hallway.

"Getting a glass of water," She answered, feeling a tide of red creep up her neck as she looked at him. His black hair was sticking out in places, probably where she'd pulled at it. A shadow of a beard covered his jaw and thankfully he was wearing a pair of black briefs that clung and moulded his hips. He had a beautiful body she now knew. Tall, lean and athletic and covered with a light dusting of dark hair. A large tribal tattoo with a Celtic symbol in the middle ran from his left armpit, twirling down his ribcage to dip into the shallow ridge of his left groin, before disappearing beneath the white elastic band of his briefs. Her cheeks grew hot, knowing she had traced every swirl with her tongue.

"Making love all night will do that to you," Teddy answered, forcing her to look at him as he walked slowly but purposely towards her and noting that his black shirt looked really sexy against her brown skin.

Teddy stepped into her space, so close that their heat mingled and teased. He took the heavy tumbler from her, bringing it to his lips and drank thirstily before putting the glass on the counter behind them.

Teddy liked playing with her. Her subtle innocence intrigued him, as now she was trying not to look at him but was in fact eating him alive. Felicity was the most beautifully gorgeous, complex woman, and he wanted more of her. Much more.

Crowding her into the small breakfast bar behind her he slid first one button through it's hole on the shirt and then the other in concentrated slowness. He left the final button at her belly button. Leaving a tantalizing V down her front.

Brushing his hands beneath the soft fabric he smoothed the skin on her shoulders. He felt her tremble. Good, he thought. Teddy skimmed his hands up and over her shoulders, making the shirt gape to her stomach. He growled deep in his throat. God she was beautiful, he thought, trying to slow down to enjoy every bit of the moment. Stepping even closer, he stroked her warm skin from her collar bone down between her breasts, down further to the shallow dip of her belly button, then up again. He trailed his fingers up and down, watching the play of his fingers against her buttery soft skin.

She whimpered, tipping her head back, giving him access to the exposed curve of her neck, leaving herself open and vulnerable but really not caring.

Teddy obliged, slowly sweeping his tongue behind her ear, down her neck and back again, nibbling on her earlobe for a moment then cupping a breast to tug at the already swollen nipple.

Fliss felt her knees giving way and clutched at the stool behind her. She raised one leg, wrapping it around Teddy's calf to keep her balance.

Teddy shifted his stance, moved down her body, lavished attention on one succulent nipple and then the other before dropping to his knees lifting her leg over his shoulder exposing her sex to him.

Fliss whimpered again, now used to the expertise of his mouth and the pleasure it would bring. He didn't disappoint. He was there, a large hand massaging one delectable cheek of her bottom, as, holding her close, she rocked into his mouth.

Teddy took everything from her, every orgasmic tremor was wrung from her to his satisfaction then he kissed her, letting her taste herself on his lips, before quickly turning her around and entering her in one smooth movement.

Together they rocked against each other. The tension building rapidly as Teddy pushed into her. He urgently wrapped a strong arm around her waist, keeping her steady as he pumped into her.

He gave her everything and her scream mingled with his deep moans as his body exploded with the intensity of his release.

"Felicity." He whispered as he lay his head between her shoulder blades and held her close. She was his.

CHAPTER SEVEN

Fliss turned her back on her team mates, pulled the hood on her green and brown Nottingham Outlaws hoodie, and closed her eyes as the rhythmic swish of the train became background noise and she purposely recalled the last twenty four hours.

Teddy had managed to get her to the hotel, but only just. He'd insisted on making her breakfast of coffee and toast with marmite. Then they'd showered together, where he'd taken his time washing her hair. All the while with an arrogant smirk on his face.

When she'd asked him about it he'd grinned and all but thumped his chest.

"Ten," he'd said smugly.

"Ten what?" Fliss remembered asking, as he'd wrapped her in a fluffy white towel picked her up and walked effortlessly to his bedroom.

"I asked you for a number last night," Teddy reminded her, blotting the excess water from her skin tenderly. "And you said ten."

"And?" She'd prompted, watching, as he'd picked up the little shimmery top she'd worn last night. She had wrinkled her nose in distaste.

Seeing the look, he'd rolled his eyes, but went to his wardrobe anyway and pulled out a black T-shirt before turning to her with a look of expectancy.

She'd grinned and nodded.

"Orgasms," he'd replied, pulling the T-shirt over her head. "You said ten, I gave you ten."

She'd giggled. "I can't believe you actually counted them," she'd chastised, pinching his arm playfully then pulling him down for a quick kiss.

"I've never had any before." Fliss had revealed, lifting her hips off the bed so he could skim her jeans over her hips.

When had she ever been so malleable, allowing a man to dress her? She remembered thinking, and why was she being so affectionate? All of this was not her. She did not roll over and do anyone's bidding.

"And I'll be the only one giving them to you." Teddy had warned, his blue eyes watching her in that probing, intent way of his.

Fliss remembered staring him down, well as much as she could being pinned beneath him. They hadn't made any promises for tomorrow and she expected nothing from him. She'd had a bite of her apple, enjoyed the hours with him, but she refused to think beyond the here and now.

Maybe he hadn't liked whatever it was he saw in her eyes, or maybe she had taken too long to answer because, with a sound deep in his throat, Teddy had pushed her jeans down to her ankles covered her mouth with his and quickly unbuckled his belt. He'd entered her tender body with almost no preliminaries but she had been ready.

Eleven became her favourite number moments later.

The team had been waiting for her. Fliss had never been so embarrassed in her life as Teddy had kissed her thoroughly, tapped her playfully on the chin, waved to everyone and was gone. Priya had sauntered over holding her weekend bag that she'd packed for her.

Felicity's embarrassment had been complete.

***

"So?"

"So what?" Fliss looked at Mackenzie. It was the first shift since their trip to London and they were both having dinner in the little room just off the main floor.

Dinner at four in the morning. Fliss kept her meals light, a small tuna pasta salad that had been on special offer at the supermarket. Mackenzie was busy heating up what looked like one of those all

46

day breakfast platters of eggs, bacon, sausages, hash browns, baked beans and even haggis. She shuddered.

"I don't know how you can eat all that at this time of the morning," she said, knowing what he wanted to talk about. He'd been dying to engage her in a conversation all through the shift, but they had been too busy.

"I don't know why you won't answer my question," he shot back, going to the drinks machine, feeding a ten pence into it and watching as it made a large black coffee for him.

"What question?" Fliss feigned interest in her pasta.

"Teddy!" Mackenzie carefully pulled his cup of coffee from the machine and held it by the rim as the paper cup itself was ridiculously hot. "That epitome of handsomeness you spent the night with and came back looking like you got a good and proper shag," he said, sitting at her table.

"Mackenzie, I really wonder about you sometimes," she said. "Are you gay?"

He looked at her, his face blank and unreadable. "Hmm, maybe," he shrugged.

"So you admit it?" Fliss persisted.

"I'll tell you if you tell me."

"Fine."

"You first."

"Teddy used to live round the corner from me."

"Blah blah blah," Mackenzie interrupted, pitching a piece of bacon with his fork and waving it around. "I know all that stuff already."

"We talked all night," Fliss edged.

"No you didn't," he smirked.

Fliss felt a tide of heat creep up her neck. "Well not all night."

He grinned at her. "Was he good?"

Fliss felt her cheeks grow even hotter, she couldn't believe she was even having this conversation.

"Actually don't answer," he held up his hand. "You were well and truly shagged out when you came back. I'm surprised you could

47

even walk." He burst out laughing.

"So are you or aren't you?" Fliss asked, when his laughter trickled to a stop and she watched fascinated as his bright eyes dimmed.

"All I'm saying is this," Mackenzie became watchful, putting down his plastic fork to sip his coffee. "I met a girl and I really like her but she thinks I spend too much time in front of the mirror. She said I must be gay."

Fliss laughed, she couldn't help it. Every reflective surface Mackenzie came across he looked at himself. He was forever primping and getting excited when a new moisturiser launched. He loved himself, loved looking after himself, was a slave to fashion and spent a fortune on tanning and hair products. Did all that make him less of a he man? She'd hate to think so.

"Maybe she doesn't want to compete?" Fliss advised, finishing her meal and leaning back.

He made a non committal sound deep in his throat. "Well are you two hooking up or not?" He asked, ignoring her statement.

Fliss shrugged. "I made no promises."

"I hear you."

They were both silent for a moment, Fliss finishing her cup of tea and Mackenzie scraping his fork across his plate trying to catch the last baked bean.

"I'm going to ask you another question and I don't want you to bite my head off okay?" Mackenzie asked wearily.

Fliss raised an eyebrow and looked at him. Was she really such a bad tempered bitch that her team mates were scared of upsetting her? "Go on then."

"How are you feeling Fliss?" He started.

Of all the questions she thought he would ask this was not it. "Fine. Why?"

"It's just that you've lost weight and you seem," he looked at her carefully. "I don't know, listless?"

"I feel fine."

"Preggers?"

"Pregnant! Don't be stupid."

He nodded, but still looked concerned. "Get yourself some vitamins or something, winter bugs are going around and you look like shit."

She laughed and saluted him. "Yes boss."

"Cheeky bitch," he joked before gulping the last of his coffee.

"You know you now owe me two drinks for swearing," she teased and laughed while he just rolled his eyes. The bet was still on and Mackenzie was the only one who was losing.

"Have you seen the latest e-mail?" Ingrid asked, coming in to the room.

"What e-mail?"

"Monica-Louise sent it."

"No," Fliss and Mackenzie said in unison.

"What does she want now?" Fliss asked. She was really tired of all the bureaucratic bull and all the stuff they had to remember. Being paperless only worked so far. There was just too much information and daily changes for them to remember. They were human beings for goodness sake, not machines.

"It's good news actually." Ingrid bought herself a can of pop, a packet of salt and vinegar crisps and a chocolate bar and sat with them. "Our floor is going to be refurbished."

"Toot toot!" Mackenzie made a pumping motion with one arm.

"At least Mr. Chandler-Wright didn't forget his promise to us," Fliss said.

"He's the one behind it?" Ingrid asked, liking their new boss.

"In that meeting I had with him," Fliss revealed, "before we knew he was involved with Della he said our floor was depressing and I agreed. He even asked what colours I would like to see and I said the brighter the better," she recalled. "He'd laughed."

"How is Della anyway?" Ingrid asked. "I do miss her. It's like our mum is missing."

"Aren't you and her the same age?" Mackenzie asked.

"No she's much older," Ingrid replied. "I just look like crap."

"Don't say that about yourself."

"I do though." Ingrid looked at her hands, noticing the dry and flaky skin and her nails torn with irregular lengths.

"Then if you feel that way do something about it," Mackenzie advised.

Ingrid looked at him sadly and dipped her head, her greasy blonde hair falling forward.

"Della?" Mackenzie reminded Fliss.

"Oh yeah, she's recovering nicely she's with our new boss and his daughter Gabbs."

"I'm just glad she's alive."

"Me too. I-"

"Felicity, your dinner ended five minutes ago!" Monica-Louise burst into the room like a tight tornado in her too short skirt, too tight blouse and cat-o-nine-tail hair extensions whipping around her shoulders. "I'm going to-"

Fliss scooped up her things, dropped them into the plastic carrier bag she had brought them in and was out of the door before Monica-Louise could finish her sentence.

CHAPTER EIGHT

"Mrs Rossington? Elizabeth? Are you there?" Fliss asked urgently, pushing the microphone broom closer to her mouth.

They had been chatting away, Fliss telling her about her trip to London, singing on stage and meeting Teddy. Mrs. Rossington had been teasing her about her love life, when Fliss heard a hissing sound, a thump and then the sound of glass breaking, then nothing.

"Mrs. Rossington!" Fliss cried. "Hold on. Please hold on!"

Without a second thought, Fliss had her mobile out and rang the emergency services, looking at her computer screen and quickly giving out her friend's address.

The operator introduced himself as Tony and calmly told her to stay on the line, the ambulance was on it's way.

"Felicity Pecora, put that phone away!" Monica-Louise shouted from her desk. "Now!"

"You shut up," Jarrett shot back, standing up. "It's an emergency!"

Those not on a call stood up to look at Fliss, seeing her as they'd never seen her before. Her face drained of all colour, her eyes dark and watery as she tried to hold back tears. Monica-Louise moved to stand beside her.

"What's your name?" Tony the operator asked.

"Felicity." Felicity could hear her own heartbeat. Someone tried to push a cup of water into her hand but she waved it away.

"Okay Felicity," Tony said. "You were talking to Mrs. Rossington on your other line?"

Felicity nodded.

"Felicity?"

"Sorry. Yes."

"Can you call out to her, see if she answers?"

"Okay."

Felicity did just that, but only heard silence.

"She's not answering."

"That's okay, the ambulance is two minutes away. Do you know if anyone lives with her?"

"She lives alone."

"Up pretty late isn't she?" Tony said conversationally.

Fliss smiled. "She hasn't been sleeping too well so rings to do a bit of late night shopping and have a chat," Fliss revealed trying to catch the sob in her throat.

"She sounds nice."

"She's lovely."

Fliss could hear him tapping away at his keyboard.

"Okay, the ambulance should be there now."

Another second and Fliss heard the melodious harmony of a door bell being rung twice and then a crash, footsteps and then shouting.

Fliss strained her ears to hear what they were saying.

"Felicity?"

"Yes Tony?"

"The paramedics are there now."

"Yes." She could hear shuffling and two men talking, but she couldn't make out what they were saying.

"They're taking Mrs. Rossington to the hospital Felicity, and will disconnect her telephone now, all right?"

"Okay." Fliss heard the dial tone in her headset and automatically punched in the three digit code for emergencies into her own phone. She pulled off the headset and placed it very carefully and very slowly onto her desk.

"If you ever want a job with us give me a ring, Tony Paddington, as in the station, Emergency Division in Newcastle. We could use someone as level-headed as you."

"Thank you," Fliss stuttered, her throat closing tight over the words. "Do you know if she's all right?"

"I'm sorry I don't," he apologised. "I'm going to hang up now. You did good Felicity."

"Thank you," she said again, as a tear trickled down her face and the line went dead. She looked at her mobile phone, seeing the photograph of her mother laughing with her head flung back. That photograph was two years old.

Someone, Mackenzie, took her mobile from her, pushed her into her chair and fed the cup of water into her hands, but her hands were shaking so badly he put the cup to her lips instead.

"Drink," he ordered. "You okay?" He asked after she had taken a sip.

Fliss shook her head and he pulled her head into the crook of his neck and rubbed her back in soothing circular motions as she cried.

"What happened?" Lucia whispered.

"Something happened to her friend whilst she was on the call. I think she collapsed or something," Mackenzie told them. "I'm taking her to the staff room." He told the floor captain who was standing pale faced watching them.

"Yes or course." Monica-Louise seemed to pull herself together. "Everyone else back on the phones please." She clapped her hands at them as though herding chickens.

"Come on Fliss." Mackenzie walked her over to the staff room and made her sit on the leather sofa and held her hand.

"What if she's dead?" Fliss asked him, as she scrubbed the tears away.

"She's not dead."

"How do you know?"

"I don't, but if she's not dead and you're already thinking she might be, might make her give up and die anyway. So she's not dead."

It took a moment but Fliss finally understood what he'd used a lot of words to say.

"She'll be ringing in a few days and placing more orders. Watch," Mackenzie said, giving her an encouraging nod.

She wanted to believe him, oh God she wanted to believe him.

"If you want to go home Felicity you can," Monica-Louise said, coming into the room.

"No I'll be okay."

"Do you want to tell me what happened?" Their floor captain asked, going to the drinks machine. She fed some change into it and got a can of high energy drink out. She handed it to Fliss.

Gratefully Fliss accepted the drink and, trying to hold back her tears, told her what had happened.

CHAPTER NINE

Teddy was pissed off. Felicity had promised she'd meet him in town today. He'd taken a few days off and was in Nottingham to see his family before Christmas, as he'd be in London over the holidays.

They'd arranged to meet at the Left Lion in Old Market Square. The lions were famous, Leo and Oscar. Lying there on either side of The Council House Building, they looked splendid in wedding photographs, watching people hustle passed doing their shopping or meeting someone. Everyone in Nottingham had met someone, at least once in their life, by the Left Lion in Old Market Square.

He'd waited, but would be damned if he was going to stand there, looking like an idiot, waiting for an hour.

They'd been speaking everyday, sometimes twice a day, and Teddy had thought they were getting to know each other. Felicity was sometimes distant and at times she got testy over the phone, but that was because she wasn't used to sharing anything of herself with anyone.

Felicity liked to give the impression that she was a bad-ass, but he knew differently. She was walking through life with a wedge of vulnerability deep within her heart. She was terrified of anyone getting too close just in case they hurt her. So she pushed, what she hadn't expected was for him to push back.

Yes Teddy was pissed off. Pissed off that she wasn't answering her damn phone either. He pushed his phone into his back pocket and shivered, not used to the seeping misty coldness of the East Midlands any more. Pulling his beanie low on his head, he shoved his hands into his coat pockets and trudged back to his car. She'd best be home, he thought darkly.

Their back gardens were separated by a narrow rubbish filled alley that no one in their right mind would use once it got dark. His street, being closer to the main road, was open and well kept, all of the houses privately owned.

The majority of houses on Fliss's street were shabby. The street not only screamed council owned, it screamed I'm a council house and the occupants don't give a toss!

Glad to see the old soggy mattress that had been in Fliss's garden for years was no longer there, Teddy knocked on the door. The kitchen was at the front but the nets were so thick he couldn't see in. A dog was barking inside.

Knocking again, he waited before turning the door handle and wasn't surprised the door swung open. Felicity's mother had run an open house, allowing any drugged up transient or runaway to stay for days on end. Pay her with cigarettes and booze and you could stay. She had no business having those types of people around her young daughter, he thought grimly. Why was Felicity still living here?

Stepping over several overstuffed bin bags, he was disgusted to see Felicity's mother lying on the sofa, her eyes closed, her legs sprawled and her dressing gown gaping. The TV was blaring an afternoon talk show where a teenager was crying and shouting DNA will prove it to a bored older man beside her.

A staffie bull terrier came up to him wagging its tail madly. Teddy patted the dog's wide head.

"Felicity here boy?" He asked the sandy coloured dog, who was trailing behind him with eyes full of devotion. Teddy looked in all the rooms downstairs, stepping over a man sleeping face down on a roll of winter coats, before going upstairs.

One bedroom had two men sleeping in it, another room was full of boxes and junk. He knocked on the third door that had 'Keep Out' notices and two heavy duty hasp and staple padlocks on it, though the padlocks looked broken.

"Felicity?" He called out, trying the handle, but the door was locked from the inside. "Fliss? It's Teddy."

The dog brushed passed his leg and started scratching at the door.

"She in here boy?" Teddy asked the dog.

The dog continued to scratch and whine quietly.

"I'm coming in." He advised. If anyone was with her he'd kill them both he thought silently. Stepping back, he kicked the door open and it slammed against the wall. The dog rushed in and jumped on the bed.

Fliss was lying crunched up in a tight ball under a thin sheet, shivering and moaning softly. The dog was licking her face and whining softly.

Teddy grabbed the dog's collar and hauled him off the bed. "Fliss?" He touched her cheek and she opened her eyes. "You sick?" He touched her forehead, she was burning up so he bent down to gather her up, but she screamed out in pain.

"What is it?" He asked in confusion, letting her go quickly. "Where hurts?"

But she'd closed her eyes.

Teddy quickly dug his phone out of his pocket and called for an ambulance.

Had she overdosed?

***

Teddy stayed by her side as the paramedics asked him questions he couldn't answer, did she do drugs they asked. He didn't think so. The looks they gave him, the neighbourhood and the condition of the house, he knew they thought otherwise. Judging him, judging her. Their postcode making them a target for unwarranted prejudice. Any other time Teddy would have pulled them up on it.

He was able to rouse her mother long enough to tell her he was taking Fliss to the hospital, but she was so out of it he doubted she'd even remember. Fliss lived like this? Why did she still live like this? He thought angrily. Why was she here?

"She went into crisis," the doctor explained later that night.

"Crisis?" Teddy asked the tall thin Asian doctor.

"Sickle cell crisis," he explained. "Miss Pecora has full-blown sickle cell. She'd had a crisis when she was eight years old and had stayed in the hospital for several weeks."

The doctor looked at him, then at the notes in his hand. "Hmm, strange," He went on. "Your fiancée has been lucky. Normally sickle cell patients are in and out of hospital until we can get them on a management programme and even then we'd see them every three months." The doctor looked down at the notes in his hand again, flicking through the few pages there. "From our records she'd been in hospital a few times when she was younger and then nothing. Has she lived abroad?"

"I don't think so," Teddy answered. "I'm sorry but what is sickle cell?" He asked, aware he'd lied to the doctor regarding his relationship to Fliss so that he could stay with her. "I've never heard of it."

"It's an inherited disease of the blood." The doctor sat on one of the plastic chairs in the dimly lit corridor and pulled a piece of paper from his pocket, drawing a few circles on it and then some shapes. He turned to show Teddy. "This is what normal blood cells look like," he indicated the circles, "and this is what a sickle cell looks like." He explained, tracing the banana shape. "When the sickle cell moves around the body they can stick together and stop parts of the body from getting oxygen. It can be excruciatingly painful. Your fiancée was in a lot of pain."

"Will she get better?" Teddy asked.

"We can manage her sickle cell but we can't cure it." He looked at his watch and stood. "You may as well go home now, I've sedated her so she'll sleep through the night and then some."

"I'm staying."

The doctor nodded in understanding before showing him another room just off the corridor with a TV, plush chairs and two vending machines.

Teddy bought himself a coffee before slumping into a chair. How long had she been in her room? The last time he'd spoken to her she'd mentioned feeling a little tired and getting over a winter bug. Did she even know she had sickle cell?

Teddy took out his phone, pulled up his search engine, typed in sickle cell and read.

"Hey." Teddy said. It was late afternoon of the next day.

Felicity was propped up in bed and, although she had multiple tubes and wires attached to her, she looked better than yesterday.

"You brought me here?" She whispered tiredly.

"You don't remember?" He moved closer and touched her fingers ever so gently, aware even now she could be hurting. He'd spent hours last night reading up and researching the disease, knowing her whole body could be throbbing in pain.

"You didn't meet me at the Left Lion," he accused with a smile. "I went round to your house and found you like this. Promise me you won't scare me like this again," he urged, bending to kiss her temple and hearing her breath catch in her throat. "Hurt?"

She nodded.

"I went shopping and bought you some stuff." He held up a paper bag with a trendy logo on it.

"Thank you."

"A nightie," he said remembering his embarrassment when he described her size to the sales-lady. "Slippers, socks, undies, it's all in here," he listed, placing the bag within easy reach for her on the bed. "Enough for a week or two."

She smiled tiredly before sliding down into the bed and cautiously turning onto her side to face him as he sat down.

"You scared the shit out of me Felicity."

"Sorry," she grimaced then smiled. "I scared the shit out of me too," she revealed. "I just thought I had a virus or something."

"You didn't know about this sickle cell thing?"

She shook her head.

"Not going into hospital when you were a kid?" He asked.

"I remember going into hospital, but not what for? My mother never said."

"Your mother has a lot to answer for!" He wanted to hit a wall and was glad her mother wasn't here right now as he could have easily throttled her. "You could have died," he went on grimly, pulling in some much needed air. "How long were you feeling like this?" He asked, trying to calm down.

"Aches and pains?" She closed her eyes, remembering her trips to the corner shop trying to convince a passer-by to buy her painkillers as she was to young to buy them herself. She remembered the increasing number of painkillers she had been taking lately as well. Fliss peeked at him under her lashes, his normally gorgeous blue eyes were shadowed, his eye whites pink with tiredness and his mouth tight, flat and pulling downwards. She didn't want to add to his distress. "Not long," she lied.

"Is there anyone you want me to ring for you?" He asked, changing the subject.

"Work, I was supposed to go in last night," she remembered. "Della, she'll be worried if she doesn't hear from me."

"Who's Della?"

"My Jamaican friend. She's a lot older than me."

Teddy watched, fascinated, as a tide of red crept up Fliss's neck.

"I love her like a mother," she revealed almost defensively. "We met at work." She turned as fast as she could to look on the bedside table. "Where's my phone?"

"I didn't see it in your room, but then I wasn't really looking for it."

"Can you get it for me?" She asked. "It might be under my pillow or on top of the wardrobe," she said, embarrassed. "Did you lock my door?" She asked anxiously.

It was a strange conversation, almost pedestrian and he reached for her hand, gently rubbing his thumb across her warm skin. He had so many questions he wanted to ask her but not today. Today was about healing. He'd failed her when she was younger, thinking the fire and angry determination in her eyes would take her away from the poverty and neglect of her upbringing. He'd been wrong and the guilt clung to him like black tar.

"No," he didn't want her worrying. "Tell me what you need me to do and I'll sort it for you." He stood up and shrugged into his coat.

"You just concentrate on getting better and leave the rest to me okay?"

She looked so young and vulnerable lying there, her brown skin pale against the white sheet. He knew how difficult it was for her to rely on anyone, it had been the same for him until he realised everyone needed someone and not everyone let you down. He and Felicity were one and the same.

"Go back to sleep," he urged, stroking her hair.

"You'll come back?" She slurred, her eyes already closing.

"I'll be here when you wake up," he promised.

***

Teddy didn't like going to his mother's house. He'd grown up in this house and had some pretty good memories, it was just that it was always so noisy.

He'd shared a room with Pauly, which was okay, because Pauly was rarely ever there and when he'd hit his teenage years had spent most of his time with the athletics club, coming home exhausted and going straight to bed.

Teddy didn't really remember his own father. He'd skipped out on them when he was four or five and went back to Ireland.

His mother was one of those women who didn't like to be alone. She'd always had a man, any man, in the house. The best one was Deck, the father of the last three boys. Deck was a stern, body building bus driver from Barbados who raised them all. Deck would be the only one Teddy would ever call Dad.

Knocking on the door, Teddy waited. Della was with Felicity so he thought now would be a good time to visit his family. If they heard he was in town and hadn't come round he wouldn't hear the end of it.

"Teddy!" Teddy found himself engulfed in two strong arms and his back being slapped several times. Deck was burly and affectionate. "We weren't expecting you for another few days." Deck stepped aside to let Teddy pass. "Iona? Iona!" Deck yelled. "Guess who's here?" Deck called up the stairs.

Teddy winced. This house was always loud. Growing up he'd hated the constant yelling, fighting between his siblings and the bloody footsteps up and down the damn stairs. Teddy had left home to get his own place as soon as he could.

"Teddy, my handsome boy." his mother came down the stairs, her black hair straight and immaculate as always. His mother had always looked after herself and Deck had always indulged her every need. She was spoilt.

Teddy found himself wrapped in his mother's arms and kissed on both cheeks. She stepped back to look at him. "Still a fine looking man. Have you got yourself a girlfriend yet?" She asked with a slight Irish lilt.

If Iona had her way she'd have him married off before Christmas, Teddy knew. He wanted to tell her about Felicity, but now wasn't the time. When Felicity was out of hospital then he'd bring her round for a visit.

"Deck, fire up the bar-be-cue!" Iona yelled into the kitchen. "We need to get some meat on his bones."

Tucking her arm through his, Teddy found himself dragged to the back of the house where Deck was already inspecting the bar-be-cue grill. He and Pauly had bought him a fancy gas one last Christmas but Deck always went back to the customised drum he'd built himself. He liked to bar-be-cue Caribbean style he'd said.

"Now tell me what you've been doing and have you seen your brother?" Iona asked as they settled around the kitchen table.

CHAPTER TEN

Fliss woke up to see a hand-tied bouquet of yellow flowers on her table and Della reading a red top newspaper beside her bed.

Long dreadlocks were tied at the back of Della's neck and a cobalt blue headscarf was wrapped around her head, covering the shaved patch of hair Felicity knew was there. Della was lucky to be alive, she'd been attacked whilst walking to her son's house several weeks ago and the attacker had stabbed her as well as cut a chunk of her hair off.

"Hey Della!"

"Hi sweetheart, don't move," Della told her, quickly folding her newspaper, putting it on top of her handbag and moving to sit on the bed. "How are you feeling?"

"A lot better than I was three days ago." Fliss replied honestly. She did feel better and had started a sickle cell management programme that seemed to be working. It was the first time in years that she didn't feel some form of throbbing pain in her back and hands. She'd had a blood transfusion yesterday and Teddy had stayed with her the whole time, she recalled warmly. "Have you been here long?"

"Half an hour or so." Della picked up her hand. "What happened Fliss?" She asked mildly.

Fliss looked at the wall, she didn't like talking about herself, but in a moment of weakness whilst Della was recovering from a stab wound in this very hospital, Fliss had talked about her life.

"I was home and couldn't get out of bed," she admitted, looking down at her fingers. "The pain was so bad, Della, I thought I was going to die." A tear slid down her cheek as she remembered the feeling of utter helplessness when nobody in the house heard her calls for help. She'd been so scared.

Della reached for her hands and tucked them within her own. "Why didn't you ring me?"

"Don't be mad," Fliss urged.

"No credit?" Della stated huffing in disgust. "I've told you countless times Felicity. How many times?" She asked.

"Countless." Felicity murmured self-consciously. Della was everything a mother was supposed to be. She told her off, she had expectations that she expected Felicity to meet and Felicity strove to meet them. Things would have been so different if Della or someone like her had been in her life earlier.

"Sorry," Felicity said.

"And so you'd better be," Della stated with a gentle smile. "I thought sickle cell was an African Caribbean disease?" She said, changing the subject. "I didn't know mixed raced people could get it."

"Apparently both my mother and my father have the trait."

"Your mother is from the Caribbean isn't she?"

"That's what she thinks. She was brought up in foster care. Dr. Guresh, he's my doctor, says it's more prevalent in African Caribbean people, but other ethnicities also carry it. It's just my bad luck my mother hooked up with my father for a night."

"What are the odds of that? Bad luck seems to be your middle name," Della said without malice. "We need to start calling you lucky and sending you positive vibes to turn your luck around, but never mind we'll get you through this," Della said cheerily. "Now, tell me about this Teddy." She urged with a smile. "He rang me this morning but wouldn't tell me anything over the phone. I had to meet him at a coffee shop before he even told me which hospital you were in!"

Teddy was protecting her and Fliss could do nothing about the heat of embarrassment that touched her cheeks. "He's my friend."

"I'm your friend, Fliss," Della said coyly. "The poor boy was out of his mind with worry and very suspicious of me until I set him straight."

"He's twenty five, hardly a boy," Fliss confirmed. "What was he like?" Fliss asked, looking at a small tear in her nail.

"Very very cautious," Della revealed. "The boy has feelings for you," Della stated, with a tinge of her Jamaican accent.

"He used to live near me and we have history that's all." Felicity shoved the image of him on his knees worshipping her body from her mind.

"Hm," Della winked knowingly. "I see that twinkle in your eye," she teased. "How long will you be here for? Any ideas?"

"Dr. Guresh said I'm responding well to the medication. The jaundice is clearing and they'll be doing some tests on my bones tomorrow, then hopefully," she crossed her fingers. "I can go home."

"Not to that house you're not."

"Della you know I have nowhere else to go."

"Spencer is taking me down to London to recuperate," she made bunny ears with her fingers.

"You don't want to go?"

"I've got no choice," Della replied. "The kids want me to go and Spencer wants me to see his house." She and Spencer had been childhood sweethearts in Jamaica, but she'd left without telling him of her pregnancy. That had been twenty years ago. He'd recently found her and to say that they had stuff to work out was an understatement.

Felicity noted that Della didn't seem too enthused about it.

"You two getting together?" Felicity asked.

"I really don't know," Della admitted, plucking a grey cat hair from her black leggings. "We'll see."

They were both lost in their own thoughts for a moment.

"How about you house-sit for me?" Della suggested.

"House-sit?"

"It'll be empty and better to have someone I trust living there."

"What about your son? Your family?"

"Isaac doesn't live with me," Della reminded her. "And he spends most of his time with Spencer's daughter Gabbs anyway."

"Okay, if you're sure?" If it was anyone else Felicity would have said no, she relied on no one but this was Della.

"I'm sure. I'll drop off some keys tomorrow," Della confirmed. "Now, any gossip from work? And what's wrong with your speech? You haven't said a single swear word since I've been here."

Felicity laughed and settled in to tell her all that had been happening since Della had been stabbed and was on sick leave.

***

Fliss was pleasantly surprised when Jarrett, Priya and Lucia entered her room talking loudly. It was a good job the only other patient was an old lady who had a bed by the window and she had her own set of noisy visitors.

"Hey guys." She really was pleased to see them. When had they begun to mean anything to her? Fliss thought. She didn't do friends.

"Hey Fliss," Jarrett said with a smile, hugging her close and kissing her cheek. "What the fuck is this all about?" He waved a hand, pointing out her being in the bed and the small ward.

"You owe me a coffee when I get back." Fliss hugged him back awkwardly.

They all laughed, remembering the team bet. The girls hugged their hellos and also kissed her.

"Good," Jarrett said, flashing his lovely teeth. "I just want to make sure you are coming back." He placed a large card on her legs.

"This is from everyone," Lucia said arranging a large bouquet of lilies in a glass vase Priya handed to her. "Oh, and Ingrid sent you this." She dug into her coat pocket and pulled out Fliss's favourite chocolate bar from the vending machine at work.

"They're lovely thank you." Feeling her eyes beginning to sting, Fliss dabbed the corners with the edge of her sheet.

"You crying Fliss?" Priya asked, unable to keep the amazement from her voice.

"Don't be stupid," Fliss answered. "I don't do such things." She finished huffily, but ruined the effect by smiling.

They all laughed.

It was a nice visit and they stayed for a while, making her laugh with all the gossip and filling her in on all the changes. They'd had to move floors temporarily as they were getting new pods, carpets, wall hangings and the brightest colours on the walls. All thanks to her they said.

"Hey your Mrs. Rossington called last night," Jarrett said quietly as he sat on the edge of Fliss's bed. "I told her you were in hospital and she wanted to send you some flowers, but you know I wasn't about to give out your personal info and stuff."

Fliss looked over at Lucia and Priya, but they were busy looking at the card and laughing between themselves over something someone had written.

"If she rings back can you give her my mobile number?"

Jarrett's jet black eyebrows dipped low. "Are you sure? You've never even met the woman."

"Who says?" Fliss challenged.

He scowled. "You haven't."

"Okay I haven't, but she's fine."

"Fliss she could be a crazy woman."

"She's not."

"How do you know?"

She shrugged. "Gut instinct?"

"I'm not giving out your number." Jarrett crossed his arms over his impressive chest.

"Jarrett please."

"She could be an axe murderer or something doggy."

"Dodgy," Fliss corrected automatically. Usually Jarrett's English was impeccable but sometimes, like now, it failed him. "She's eighty six."

"So? Old people kill all the time."

"Like who?"

"Fliss," he warned. "It's dangerous."

She crossed her arms and looked at him with narrowed eyes. "If you don't do it, I'll tell her," she rolled her eyes in the direction of Lucia. "That you like her."

Their eyes clashed, darkest brown versus golden brown.

"You play dirty Felicity."

"I want what I want when I want it," she replied smugly. "Well?"

"Tell you what," he sighed. "I'll give her your e-mail. That's safer."

"Fine," she rattled it off watching, as Jarrett put it in his phone. "Thank you."

He put his phone away.

"You're welcome."

"Have you told her yet?"

"Problem with the other one."

It was as though they were speaking in code, but Fliss remembered the hot glances Monica-Louise sent his way and how he used to encourage them.

"It'll sort itself out." Fliss would love if he and Lucia got together. He was just too nice for a woman like Monica-Louise. She'd eat him alive.

He grinned. "Now tell me about your boyfriend Teddy."

"He's not my boyfriend." Fliss stated and flushed to the roots of her hair as Teddy himself walked into the room and by the set of his jaw she knew he'd heard.

CHAPTER ELEVEN

"What would you call me then Felicity?" Teddy asked eventually.

It was much later and everyone but Teddy had gone. Fliss had been on tenterhooks watching him interact with her friends, very much aware that his blue eyes just weren't as bright and friendly when he looked at her.

Contrary to popular belief, Fliss enjoyed every meal they brought her in hospital. Tonight it was thinly sliced roast beef and potatoes and a lemon sorbet for dessert. Teddy also got a tray as he'd taken to laughing and chatting with the nurses and they'd taken to him, giving him a tray from the trolley. It was a win win situation, he'd joked as the nurses gushed about how lovely he was to Fliss and how lucky she was to be marrying such a charmer. She didn't feel the least bit lucky, she thought darkly.

Dr. Guresh had come by to see how she was doing after dinner and Teddy had asked about her aftercare once she was released from hospital, as though he had that right Fliss thought uncharitably. When she'd been about to say something, Teddy had flashed her a warning look and she'd remained mute until the doctor had left.

"I'd call you my friend," Fliss finally answered, feeling at a disadvantage lying low in the bed so rearranged her pillows and sat as high as she could. "What else?"

He sent her a withering look that spoke volumes of everything but which gave her absolutely nothing as he stood at the bottom of her bed with his hands gripping the rail.

Fliss looked at him from under her lashes. He looked good in black jeans, a ribbed jumper the colour of winter blue and a black sports coat.

"I guess we're still figuring it out." Fliss reached for the duvet Teddy had brought for her as she'd been really cold one night and pulled it up to her chin.

"I guess we are," He confirmed quietly.

Fliss could hear the nurses talking in the corridor.

"So you're my fiancée?" She asked belatedly.

"It's what I told them when I brought you here."

"So you lied?"

His blue eyes chilled. "Do you want me to leave Felicity?" He asked, moving to sit beside the bed. "Be honest with me."

She was getting better, she was almost up and about and her body didn't hurt at all. Dr. Guresh had said she might be able to go home tomorrow.

"I'm leaving soon," she edged.

"That's not what I asked," he said softly, looking at her hands clenched tightly on top of the sheet. "Do you know what I think?"

She was about to answer but he reached for her hands, loosened her fingers and threaded his fingers through hers.

"I think you're afraid," he smiled grimly. "You think you've lost control of the situation and are pushing me away." He looked at her, capturing her guilty gaze. "Push as hard as you want Felicity Pecora, but I'm staying."

Tears welled up and tipped onto her cheeks.

"I care about you," he whispered honestly. He knew it was too early in their relationship to talk about commitment but she was running scared. She was trying to pick an argument so he would leave and go back to London. Tough! He thought, he was sticking around.

"You do?" She sniffed.

"I do," he smiled tenderly, turning to sit on her bed to play with her fingers. Her nails were pink and shaped into neat ovals. There was a small plaster where the IV had been. "I've never enjoyed being around a woman as much as I do you. You're special to me." He finished.

Using his thumbs Teddy brushed her tears away. "Don't be

70

afraid," he urged. "It's time to let me in. Let me look after you."

Fliss looked at their hands clasped tightly together and she let his go. "You know this is hard for me," she admitted, plucking a small ball of lint from the green duvet. "I don't like people and they don't like me," she looked at him looking for a reaction but saw none. "And I've never done the whole girlfriend boyfriend thing before either." She revealed, knowing she sounded young and vulnerable but couldn't help it.

Teddy shook his head. "A lot of people care about you Felicity. You've had visitors every day," he pointed out with a small smile. "You're smart, beautiful and strong," Teddy listed. "You've gone through, and seen, more than you should." He picked up her hand again. "You don't like people because they've let you down but I won't. I want to see you laugh and try new things. I want to show you how wonderful and fun life can be. Let me be that person Felicity."

Their hands were wrapped into a tight fist and Teddy brought it to his lips, kissing her knuckles. He'd said all those things because they were true. Seeing her on his little stage all those weeks ago had blown him away. He remembered her upbringing, he remembered the unstable dirty environment she'd lived in. He remembered her alcoholic mother. But he'd also heard the sadness tinged with hope in her voice as she sang. He'd wanted to sweep her up and whisk her away and fill her life with nothing but happiness.

Fliss took a deep, shaky breath; she knew what he was asking. She never relied on anyone, ever. She lived her life expecting nothing from anyone. Could she even take a chance? What was it Mrs. Rossington had said to her? Live your life without regrets, take it without apology. If she didn't take this chance with Teddy, she may regret it for the rest of her life. If she told him to go she knew he would never be back. Did she really want that? She'd trusted him enough with her body, doing things with him she would never dream of doing with anyone else. He'd cherished her that night and continued to cherish her.

On another breath she nodded.

***

"And where are you off too?" Teddy asked, closing his car door and walking towards her.

Fliss felt that damnable flush singe her cheeks, she'd been caught with her coat on, her bag slung across her chest and Della's front door wide open. It was just her luck that he'd come back early. He'd left a note saying he'd be back later that evening. It was early afternoon.

He was twirling his keys around one finger, his dark eyebrows raised over eyes twinkling with amusement as she looked so guilty. "Come on," he said lightly. "Let's get something to eat."

Fliss sagged in relief. She'd been cooped up in the house for days, add the hospital stay and it added up to almost two weeks. She desperately needed some fresh air.

He locked the front door and helped her into his car. Fliss hadn't paid much attention to his vehicle. It was big, black, had deep red leather seats, glossy panels with a dashboard that looked like a pilot would have difficulty using.

"Where to?" He asked.

"Anywhere." Fliss shrugged, she wasn't dressed to go anywhere special.

"Lets go to West Bridgford I heard they have some good restaurants over there."

He started the car and turned it expertly onto the narrow street already clogged with cars.

"So where were you off to?" He asked casually.

"Home."

"Why?"

"I need to check on things and my mother," she said almost defensively.

"I stopped by yesterday."

"You never said."

"You were sleeping when I got in remember?"

"Don't keep things from me Teddy," she burst out. "It's my house and my mother. She's my responsibility!"

"Relax," he reached over to gently stroke her denim clad thigh. "I'm sorry, I should have told you this morning but I got distracted." He flashed her a quick smile before concentrating on the road again.

Fliss frowned, trying to remember what happened that morning, then flushed. She'd finished her shower and, wrapped in a towel, bumped into him in the hallway. She'd stumbled to a stop seeing his naked chest and sleepy eyes. He was staying in Della's second bedroom. They'd gotten hot and heavy kissing and touching right there. He'd been on his knees and she'd been clutching at his hair as he brought her to an energy draining orgasm. He'd then put her to bed. This was the first time she'd seen him since.

"I'm sorry too," she turned to face him. "I'm used to looking out for her by myself that's all and I've never been gone this long."

"I understand. She's fine. Those two blokes were cooking dinner and she was sleeping on the sofa."

"She didn't talk to you?"

"She was out of it." Teddy took his frustration out on the steering wheel, gripping it tightly. Her mother was always out of it. "I can't tell you not to visit, but let me take you, okay?"

"Fine."

"Felicity."

"Yes okay, fine."

"I don't like the look of those two blokes. Who are they anyway?"

"Eddy and TT?" She laughed. "They come and go every couple of weeks."

"From where?"

"I don't know."

"You've never thought to ask?"

"What would be the point?"

His knuckles turned white on the steering wheel but he kept his voice light. "The point being your safety for one."

She laughed. "They've been coming since I can remember. I think they were in the circus or something."

Teddy said nothing. Everything he wanted to say about her

household would probably hurt her feelings. Their relationship was just beginning and not for the first time he thought that maybe, just maybe, she was too young and not ready. But the thought of Felicity out there in the world all exposed and vulnerable to other men made his stomach clench. She needed him to protect her.

**

Teddy was on a mission to show her as much of the countryside as he could in the weeks that followed. She tired easily so they went for long drives where she could doze easily in the car if she needed to.

She hadn't known the East Midlands was so beautiful, to her it was just a place, a cold concrete place without much of a soul.

Now? Now she was seeing it in a different light. The different accents from people who lived barely twenty kilometres apart who could barely understand each other was fascinating. All the fields and hills, not to mention the many castles. She'd seen them all.

Fliss loved it.

She looked at Teddy, his face relaxed in his sleep.

Her sleep pattern was still out of sync, so she spent much of the night watching him, imprinting his every expression on her heart. She knew she loved him but hadn't told him. Neither had he said the words and she was okay with that.

She had things to sort out, her mother for one, and the whole situation. Being diagnosed with sickle cell meant she had to look after herself better, if she was going to get them out of that house and her mother off that sofa, she needed to get better.

Where Teddy fit in, she didn't know. All she knew was that she was taking things one day at a time.

CHAPTER TWELVE

Felicity sat bolt upright. "Fuck me," she gasped. "I have an email from Mrs. Rossington!" Swinging her bare legs off Teddy's thighs, she sat up straight, grasping her phone as she scrolled through her email reading excitedly.

"Is that the lady you saved?" Teddy reached out to rub that tantalising bit of skin between her shorts and vest top.

Felicity flapped her hands waving him away as she read.

"Oh she's okay," Fliss said, smiling through her tears.

"Here, read." She ordered, and watched keenly as Teddy read.

To my dearest friend Felicity

Felicity you have blessed me with your presence in my life and I will be forever grateful my final years have you in them.

How very strange it is my dear that a random telephone call led to this chain of events.

You saved my life. I cannot thank you enough for thinking as quickly as you did. My heart got a little tired of beating for the past eighty seven years and had a little hiccup.

Luckily you and I were talking and even when I was on the floor I could hear you telling me to hold on and calling the ambulance. I knew I just needed to hold on for a little bit longer and they would be here.

I'm still in hospital as I hurt my hip when I fell but otherwise I feel much better.

I was so perturbed to hear that you yourself have been ill. I'm an old woman and it is expected once in a while but you are young and vibrant. I do hope that you are well Felicity.

I would like to send you some thank you flowers.

Take care.
Your friend.
Alive and still dancing.

Elizabeth. x

"Are you going to reply?"

"Of course," Felicity answered without hesitation, her brows furrowing. "She's my friend."

"You've never met her."

"We've been talking for weeks," this conversation had remnants of her conversation with Jarrett in hospital, Fliss thought with annoyance. She didn't like to justify her actions to anyone. "She's a harmless old lady and my friend. I'm so glad she's okay."

"I'm glad she is too." Teddy pulled her back and rearranged her on the sofa, trapping her in his arms and forcing her to look up at him. "Now, are we going to talk about your language?"

Felicity grinned up at him, so happy the gold specks in her eyes were glowing. "I'm working on it," she admitted.

Teddy tried to scowl but ruined the effect by catching her bottom lip between his teeth and nibbling gently. "Every time you curse I'm going to kiss you stupid."

"That's my punishment?" She challenged, as she moved beneath him so that his body slipped between the V of her legs.

"Uh huh."

"Well in that case I'll curse in my head and tell you about it at night."

He chuckled and smoothed a hand down her side then up under her top to mould her naked breast in his palm.

Much later, Felicity crept downstairs and searched for her phone. It had slipped between the cushions on the sofa. Sitting down, Fliss re-read the email from her friend and hit reply.

She told Mrs. Rossington about her stay in hospital and how Teddy hadn't left her side since. She told her a little bit about her sickle cell and the management programme she was on and before she could over think it, she also added her address.

***

"I've got to go," Teddy stated.

"Go?" Felicity knew it was coming, Teddy had a business to run and couldn't stay in Nottingham indefinitely, but she had refused to think past each day. "When?"

"Later today," he shrugged. "After the morning rush hour then I'll hit the M1."

She looked at him then, walking barefoot towards her with his coffee. He was wearing a pair of grey sweats that rode low on his hips and she couldn't help but track his tattoo, inevitably feeling her nipples harden as the sexy ink disappeared below his waistband. He still looked sleepy she thought, as, in his own words, he didn't do conversation until after his second cup of coffee. She on the other hand was up with the birds.

"I left Pauly in charge but he has stuff he needs to do. He sent me a text this morning." He explained, placing her bare legs across his thighs in what was fast becoming their favourite position on the sofa.

"I understand." Fliss needed to sort herself out, get back to work and put in for some overtime. She needed to stop lazing about playing house. She had plans.

Teddy tracked his forefinger up and down her smooth shin. "I want you to come with me,"

"To London?"

"No to the moon," he teased.

"But I have work and I've got to go home."

"You're on sick leave and your mother is fine."

"My mother is not fine." She shot back, about to move her legs, but Teddy held them down with one large hand.

Teddy was tired of the same argument. "What do you want me to say Felicity?"

"I can't leave her, especially over Christmas."

It always came back to her mother. He admired Felicity's loyalty. God knows her mother didn't deserve a daughter like her. But he needed to keep an eye on her health. Felicity put everyone, her mother, he amended, ahead of herself. She was on a management program for her sickle cell but that didn't mean she wouldn't go back into crisis. She didn't know what her triggers were yet. All sickle cells carriers had one or two triggers that could make them go into crisis. Cold weather, smoking and infections were to be avoided. Luckily she'd seen sense and stopped smoking, but the image of her curled up in her bed moaning in agony would stay with him forever. He needed to make sure she took her folic acid everyday and not stress herself out and something needed to be done about her home life.

Teddy found and traced a small puckered scar just below her ankle bone. "How did you get this?" He asked, changing the subject, he had a few hours to convince her to come with him anyway.

Felicity bent her leg to see what he was looking at and remembered.

There had been two potatoes left in the house and her mother was sleeping on the sofa. Felicity had decided to make dinner. She'd filled the frying pan with oil and, leaving the skins on, chopped up the potatoes using a table knife. Standing on a chair, she'd scraped the chunks of potato into the fat and screamed in pain as the oil spat and splashed down her skirt, melting her pink plastic jelly shoes to her skin. Her mother had woken up and put her in a bath filled with cold water. That evening they'd gone out for chicken nuggets and ice cream.

"I don't remember," Felicity lied easily, getting up to put away her mug. "Are you ready for breakfast now?" They'd taken to having a beverage on the sofa and planning their day before actually having breakfast.

"The coffee is all I'm having," he replied, going to the small galley kitchen after her. She looked beautiful, he thought, with the morning sun behind her and golden brown skin looking healthy and smooth. He loved everything about her body, her curves fit into him perfectly. "Will you come with me?"

"I can't leave her for so long," she stepped to him and wrapped her hands around his waist to play in the two shallow dents at his lower back. "How about I come down on those *inbetweeny* days?"

"*Inbetweeny* days?" He frowned down at her not understanding.

"After Christmas but before New Years?"

He would have preferred the entire week, but was happy enough to get a few days. He tucked her head under his chin and pulled her even closer, moving his hands to cup her bottom and pull her into his arousal. "Deal." He grinned, dipping his head to kiss her.

CHAPTER THIRTEEN

The last time Felicity had been at St. Pancras train station she'd been trailing tiredly behind her team mates, having foolishly worked until eight o'clock that morning.

She had feigned nonchalance but it had in fact been the first time she had ever been on a train and containing her excitement had been draining.

Now it didn't matter. She stood in the historic station, surrounded by travellers speaking different languages, looking as wide eyed and appreciative at the architecture as she was.

Teddy had told her to wait for him just outside the coffee shop, so here she was waiting with nervous anticipation and missing the looks of admiration she herself was receiving.

She had been busy over the last few days doing things she had never done before. Her hair treated and trimmed, with not a curl in sight, hung straight to her shoulders in a glossy honey-gold curtain of health and vitality.

She looked at her hands and smiled, never failing to feel a thrill at her pink *oh-so-girly* nail polish with decorative glitter at the tips. She'd also been clothes shopping. Not spending a huge amount, but enough so as not to embarrass herself.

Before Teddy had come along she'd lived in jeans, trainers and tracksuits. Being on the night shift meant they didn't need to adhere to the normal work-wear policy, so one step up from pyjamas was all she wore, and when she wasn't working she was sleeping so there really hadn't been a need for glamorous clothes.

Taking her phone out she checked the time. Where was Teddy? The train had been on time but she was nervously aware she didn't even know his address.

Then she saw him, walking towards her with his hands behind his back, black jeans, his coat open showing his navy jumper with a touch of white T-shirt peeking out at his throat.

He was smiling and her heart raced with every step he took. She really wanted to run to him, fling her arms around him and hold on tight but didn't want to seem too eager, so pushed one hand into her coat pocket and the other to rest on the handle of her suitcase with studied casualness.

He was finally in front of her, his blue eyes shining bright with all he wasn't saying. He stepped closer, watching her intently but dipping ever so slightly to rest his forehead against hers. She heard him sigh and a wave of peacefulness settled around them. Then he kissed her.

It wasn't a *hello-we-are-in-a-public-place* kind of kiss, this was *I-want-to-be-in-our-bed* type of kiss. Felicity held on to his arms and sank into him.

She told him everything she wouldn't say out loud with the subtle pressure of her lips and each sweep of her tongue.

"Hello," Teddy said, eventually coming up for air, his forehead the only place touching her again.

"Hello."

Then he stepped back, took a breath and presented her with a posy of flowers.

Felicity looked down at them. White roses and tiny purple flowers she couldn't name were surrounded by soft, cream tissue paper. She had never been given anything so pretty. She sniffed.

"Hey," using his thumb and forefinger he lifted her chin seeing her eyes swimming with tears before tipping over onto her cheeks, he wiped them gently away with his thumbs.

"I'm sorry," she sniffed self consciously but smiling through her tears as she accepted the posy. "I've never been, it's just that—" she tried to explain but Teddy hugged her close, squashing the flowers between them. "Thank you." She finished lamely, burying her face in the delicate petals.

"Come on let's go." Teddy grabbed her suitcase with one hand and ushered her to the exit. "I like the hair," he acknowledged, stopping to button up her coat before they left the building to get a taxi.

"How're you feeling?" Teddy asked, as he helped her into a taxi.

"Fine," she said automatically but, seeing his pointed look admitted. "A little tired."

"God I missed you," he pulled her closer into the crook of his arm. "You can say it you know?"

"Say what?" Felicity asked snuggling into him.

"Repeat after me," he ordered. "Teddy I really missed you and can't wait to get you home to present my gorgeous naked body to you."

Felicity giggled and pinched his arm. "I have missed you."

"And the part about your body?"

"You know it's yours," she confessed shyly.

Who was this woman, Felicity thought, she had never been flirtatious or an *'I want to please you'* type of person but she was with Teddy. She wanted to take care of him.

She looked down at her hands seeing her dainty nails. Was this who had always been inside? A softly feminine person? A lover of pink? Needing the care and attention of a good man to help her become who she was meant to be?

***

At his flat Teddy stood at the threshold and opened the door with a flourish.

Felicity gasped.

There in the centre of the room stood a slightly bedraggled Christmas tree, completely naked of any ornaments, its subtle pine scent an invitation to celebrate and dress up.

Felicity fought the lump in her throat again as she stared at it, noting the bags of decorations and the stool placed right there at the front. He'd remembered, even her wanting a tree so tall she'd need a stool to decorate it. He'd remembered that little detail. It meant so much to her. Oh God, she thought, I'm falling even deeper in love.

Hugging, kissing and laughing, Felicity eventually flung off her coat and was about to get started when Teddy pulled her back and walked her to his bedroom.

"Take a nap first," he pulled her jumper over her head and reached round to unclasp her bra.

"Bu—" Felicity looked passed him to the tree in the other room.

"It'll still be here in an hour," he told her indulgently as though placating a child. "Okay?"

Toe-ing off her boots and tugging down her jeans she slid into his bed fighting a yawn.

"Okay."

***

Leaning against the door frame, Teddy watched Felicity getting ready. This was the first time they'd seen each other in almost a month and he couldn't get enough of just watching her do simple things around his flat. Now here she was peering into the mirror drawing black eye-liner on her eye lids with concentrated steadiness as they prepared to go out.

She'd changed so much over the past few months, he mused, watching her affectionately. Her fiery argumentative nature, although still there, just wasn't the first impression you got from her any more. She sang karaoke and helped out at his pub, talking to everyone whilst pulling pints and debating the lifestyle of overpaid footballers compared to other athletes. His regulars loved her.

He'd taken her to Parque Das Nacoes, his favourite city in Portugal for a long weekend, where she'd opened up even more displaying a keen sense of adventure and thirst for other cultures. He wanted to show her the world.

She didn't do so much overtime now either, respecting the restrictions of her sickle cell, getting plenty of rest and making better lifestyle choices. She was blooming and he was seriously considering asking her to move in with him, as three days out of every week twice a month wasn't enough for him any more.

"You're making me very self conscious standing there looking at me like that," Fliss said, as she used a piece of tissue to correct the line she'd drawn.

"It's been weeks since I've seen you," Teddy admitted, coming into the room with just a towel wrapped around his waist to lay on the bed.

"Oh no you don't mister!" Fliss warned, turning to face him and catching his heated gaze as it tracked down her body. "We're going out."

Teddy laughed indulgently. "Fine, but we aren't staying long." he reached for one of her curls, pulled it and watched in amusement as it bounced back into a cute spiral. "You will get a headache before midnight," he warned, reaching over to curl an arm around her waist and dragging her over to him.

"You can get the headache," she amended, sliding a quick glance at him. "Aren't you going to get ready? Pauly is expecting us in under an hour." Fliss reminded him, feeling the hard ridge of his arousal against her thigh. But Teddy swept one hand down her cream bandage dress, tugged it up to her waist and kissed her instead of answering.

Teddy growled a moment later. "No panties?"

"Of course I'm wearing panties," she replied, incensed.

Teddy mapped both hands across the smooth globes of her bottom, seeking then finding the thin lace between her firm cheeks.

He grinned up at her as he rolled them both over so she was now beneath him and kissed her hungrily.

"Got to have you," Teddy admitted thickly as he tugged his towel aside and reached across for the condom he knew he'd left on the bedside table.

***

"The condom broke," Teddy stated as, now dressed, he walked back into the bedroom some time later.

Felicity, who was again fixing her make-up, turned to look at him in shock, she could literally feel the blood leave her face.

"I promise you," Teddy took her hands, "if anything happens, I will be there for you both." He promised, looking into her eyes now dark and unreadable. "I won't let you down."

Tugging her hands free, Fliss pressed her fingers into her stomach. Pregnant. She couldn't get pregnant, had never wanted to be pregnant. She scrambled to her feet.

"Felicity?" Teddy reached for her. "Fliss?" He tried again but she pushed him away, clapped her hands over her mouth and rushed into the bathroom. He heard the swish of the key turning in its lock.

CHAPTER FOURTEEN

"Open the door damn it!" Teddy yelled, sliding his palm against the wooden panel in frustration. Felicity had been in there too long. He'd heard her retching, the toilet flushing, water running and then nothing. Nothing but silence for five minutes.

"I'll break it in," he challenged. "You know I will." Teddy threatened, stepping back to kick the door open but paused mid stride as he heard the key twist in the lock and then Felicity stepped out.

Teddy had never seen her look so miserable, her face stained with tears and her eyes red rimmed and puffy.

"Come here," he opened his arms inviting her in and held his breath as he saw her indecision. He went to her instead and hugged her close, relaxing when her arms crept around his waist hugging him.

"It'll be all right," Teddy soothed, rubbing her back.

"I can't get pregnant Teddy," she whispered into his neck.

"You'd make a great mother," he encouraged, smiling into her hair and picturing little versions of her hugging his knees.

"No I won't. My plans do not include this," she stepped back to wave a hand at him and his flat, "or babies." She finished.

Teddy didn't like what she was implying. What did he mean to her?

"It's a little early to be talking like this," he joked, desperate to lighten the mood. Maybe he shouldn't have said anything. But with her sickle cell she would need extra care if she became pregnant and the earlier a pregnancy was confirmed the better it would be for her health, he reasoned.

She'd moved to the other side of the room, her cream dress showing her curves and Teddy had to drag his eyes away from her chest where she'd crossed her arms before looking at him coldly.

"I'm never having children, yours or anyone else's." She revealed, raising her chin.

"What?" The image of her pregnant with another man's child made his anger bubble to the surface. "The thought of having my child is that repulsive to you?"

"It's not like we're going to be the happily ever after couple now is it?"

Teddy mirrored her stance and crossed his arms. "And why not?"

"I can only do one day at a time Teddy. No tomorrows. No future." She revealed, trying to keep all emotion from her voice. *One day at a time* had always been her motto, it's what got her through each day. "I've got nothing but sex to give you Teddy."

"We do more than have sex Felicity." He couldn't believe they were having this conversation and he tracked her to the bedroom but stopped. "What are you doing?"

"Leaving."

"Running." He shot back. "Put the bag down Felicity." He finished quietly.

"No," she grabbed a handful of clothes. "I'm going home."

"Put the fucking bag down!" Teddy yanked her bag off the bed and flung it into the living room. "We haven't got time for this bullshit." He took a deep breath, trying to calm down. Seeing her packing scared him. "We'll talk about this later. Pauly is going to announce his engagement tonight and you are going to smile and sparkle and be happy for them." He listed, throwing down the gauntlet.

"What would be the point?" She challenged, turning to face him.

"The point being," Teddy seethed. "We have spent the greater part of four months together!" He reminded her. Didn't he mean anything to her? Was he that easy to walk away from? "Now stop acting spoilt and start behaving like the adult you are!"

Felicity pulled herself up to her full height. "How dare—"

"Don't even bother," he cut in savagely with a slash of his hand. "Tonight is about Pauly and Becks," he began. "He likes you and wants you to be there for his announcement." Teddy reached for his jacket. "But it's your choice."

***

Neither said a word in the taxi ride to the Italian restaurant, but they both pinned smiles on their faces as the hostess escorted them to a large table shielded by an array of feathery foliage.

"Hey!" Teddy exclaimed with surprise seeing all his brothers sat watching them, grinning. "What's all this?" He said after all the back slapping and manly shoulder hugs had finished.

"Thought we'd surprise ya," Timothy, one of the twins replied eyeing Felicity. "Who's this?" He stepped back stroking his chin to openly admire her.

"Your playmate." Teddy replied looping an arm around Felicity's waist and pulling her into his side.

Timothy looked at him in confusion. "Playmate?"

"I'm Felicity." She held out her hand to her old friend. Growing up, Timothy and Callum were the only other mixed raced children she knew. Losing their friendship had sent her into a tailspin of loneliness. "Fliss Pecora?" She repeated expectantly.

Again Timothy shrugged but took her hand and brought it to his lips anyway. "It's my pleasure," he bowed low.

"It'll be my pleasure seeing my boot up your backside if you don't back off!" Teddy warned darkly, brother or not he was in no mood for Timothy and his jokes.

"Stop it." Fliss pulled away from Teddy. "He's only playing." She argued on Timothy's behalf.

Laughing, Timothy looped his own arm around her waist very much the way Teddy had done and grinning, wriggled his eyebrows at her. "No I'm not Felicity Pecora."

Teddy watched darkly as a tinge of pink touched Felicity's cheeks.

"I know you!" Callum the other twin joined in. "You used to live on that other street. You have the crazy mother."

"Cal," Teddy warned.

"It's okay," Fliss said to Teddy, her mother had been called worse. "That's me." She confirmed, finding herself the target of two very good looking males. Three, if she were to include Teddy but he was scowling at her.

"I remember you," Callum went on enthusiastically coming around the table to stand next to her, somehow shouldering Teddy out of the way. "We used to go looking for conkers and played Truth or Dare on the old train tracks in Bulwell."

Fliss laughed when Callum hugged her tightly and pulled her away from Teddy completely to sit with him and his twin. They'd obviously made up and were friends again she thought, remembering they'd fallen out over a girl last year.

Teddy sipped his drink and looked down the long table at Felicity as she laughed and chattered with his brothers as though she hadn't just ripped his heart out not even an hour ago.

"You have it bad bro."

"What?" Teddy turned to Pauly, frowning.

"Felicity there," Pauly nodded down the table. "I thought I was the lovesick one," he looked across at Becks who was talking to Lewis and Keegan their younger brothers. "But you beat me to it."

"Yeah," was all Teddy said, then mentally shook himself out of his dark mood, this was Pauly's night after all. "So what's this announcement you want to make?" Teddy asked, although he could make a good guess looking over at Becks. "Ouch!" Teddy said at the unexpected kick from Pauly under the table.

"I'll make it when I'm good and ready." Pauly said, picking up a spoon and twirling it around.

"Fine."

"Sorry we're late!" Iona, their mother walked in with Deck the father of the last three boys and the best dad out of all of them Teddy knew. He came from St. Lucia and had brought them all up as his own. "But I forgot my purse and we had to go back to the hotel."

Pauly had enough bedrooms for them all to stay but their mother preferred to do her own thing and stay in a hotel with Deck.

"How is everybody?" She asked, after kissing Teddy and Pauly and Becks and smiling a welcome to Felicity.

"Hungry!" The twins and the younger brothers said in unison.

They all laughed and contented Teddy pushed the argument with Felicity aside and concentrated on enjoying the visit with his family.

***

After a hearty dinner and congratulations on Pauly and Becks engagement they all lazed around catching up with each other.

Teddy watched his mother all animated and happy as she talked to Becks. His mother liked nothing better than to have her family all together and he wondered if she would be as welcoming to Fliss if she were to join the family.

Fliss was nervous. Teddy's mother was making her way around the table and she knew she didn't recognise her. Fliss herself hadn't seen Iona in years but she hadn't changed much. She was still beautiful with straight jet black hair to her shoulders, pale skin and the same twinkling blue eyes that Teddy had inherited.

"Who's girlfriend are you then?" Iona asked, sitting down beside her.

Her voice had the huskiness of a smoker, Fliss thought.

"That sounded very rude, didn't it?" Iona apologised, placing her hand on Fliss's arm in a comforting manner. "It's just that I can't keep up with them all," she laughed. "The twins had fallen for the same girl last year, awful thing it was," she revealed with her slight Irish accent. "Lord, I better shut up," she grimaced. "My foot keeps going into my mouth doesn't it?" She laughed again.

"It's okay," Fliss soothed. "I came with Teddy."

Iona looked down the table to her son and then back at her. "With my Teddy you say?"

Fliss sat up straighter as the older woman looked her up and down.

"Aye I see. My Teddy always keeps things to himself. I didn't even know he was seeing anyone."

Iona accepted the coffee that had been placed in front of her and reached for the small basket of sugar sachets, choosing a brown Fair Trade one.

"My boys have got me off the white sugar," Iona went on conversationally as she tore open the packet and poured in the sugar. "And onto this brown stuff or honey but it's an acquired taste is it not Fiona?"

"Felicity." Fliss corrected automatically, used to people mistaking her name for the popular Fiona.

Stirring her coffee slowly Iona turned to look at her, her blue gaze sharpening. "Felicity you say?"

Fliss nodded with a sinking heart.

"Where are you from Felicity?" The other woman asked, her voice lacking all previous warmth.

"Not—"

"She's from Nottingham Mam," Timothy chimed in, unaware of the sudden tension between the two women. "Back of our street."

The spoon Iona was holding clattered onto the table. "I'm sitting here with that whores daughter?" She snarled, her eyes narrowing as she stood up to glare at them all.

Everyone around the table stopped talking.

"Mother?" Pauly asked in confusion.

"Theodore?" Iona swung to Teddy. "You dare bring this bitch to my table? Eating with my boys!" She yelled at him. "Get her away from me!" She stumbled towards Deck who was now looking as shocked as the rest of them. "Deck get her out of here!"

Fliss picked her bag up from the floor. "I'd better go," She mumbled, without looking at any of them.

"Get her away from my boys Deck." Iona ordered hysterically. "And you!"

From the corner of her eye Fliss could see the older woman fling herself at Teddy, thumping his chest, her hair flying everywhere as he stood frozen.

"How could you Teddy! How could you sleep with that girl? She comes from scum. Her mother is scum! You'll need a shot for

91

rabies!"

Fliss ignored all calls for her to wait and raced out of the restaurant without her coat.

She ran down the street, blindly crossing one road and then another with eyes awash with tears until she spotted a taxi rank, jumped the line and got into the car.

She didn't know where to go and the driver was waiting for an address. She couldn't go back to Teddy's flat and she wouldn't get a train at this time of night either. Digging into her bag for her phone she called Della.

***

Teddy was gutted, there was no other word to describe the feeling of rot in his stomach. His mother had plunged in a knife and gutted everything out of him.

"Here." Pauly put another shot glass in his hand and he knocked the contents back. Teddy didn't know when they had got to his flat, what time it was or how many shots he'd already had. All he knew was the memory of his mother spitting ugly words and crying hysterically at him would stay with him forever.

"Do you know where she is?" Pauly asked, lining up a row of shots for them both.

Normally not a heavy drinker, Teddy picked up another glass and gulped the liquid down, feeling it blaze a path and pool heavily in his stomach burning him raw. He turned to look at his brother with unmasked anguish.

"How could this be Pauly?"

"I don't know mate," Pauly answered grimly, it was worse than bad. There were no words of comfort he could even offer. There was nothing they could do about it. "Lend me your phone. Let me try and ring her again," Pauly offered. He'd been trying to reach Fliss for over an hour but the calls kept going straight to voicemail.

Teddy passed his phone over, seeing the photo of him and Fliss laughing as they posed with their heads together with the Christmas tree in the background. They'd been so bloody happy. How could this happen?

Pauly pulled up her number again and waited, not really expecting her to answer.

"Fliss?" He jerked upright. "It's Pauly," he began. "Are you okay?" He looked at Teddy who was watching him keenly. "Yes he's here. Do you want to speak to him?" But Pauly grimaced as Teddy shook his head and made sharp negative slashes with his hands. "Actually you'd better not, he's a bit worse for wear," Pauly apologised as he tried to decipher what his brother was now telling him. "Where are you?" He asked at Teddy's nod. "With a friend? Which friend?" He asked, knowing Fliss didn't know many people in London. He looked at Teddy whilst he listened to what she was saying. "Yes I'll tell him," he confirmed. "Bye Fliss. Fliss!" He shouted before the call disconnected, "I'm sorry." He finished.

"Where is she?" Teddy demanded.

"At Della's house."

They'd had dinner with Della and Spencer a few times. At least she was safe, Teddy thought.

"How did she sound? What did she say?"

"She sounded as though she'd been crying," Pauly told him reluctantly. "But she was more interested in how you were and to tell you that she was sorry to come between you and Mam." Pauly flicked him a glance. "What are you going to do?"

"I don't know Pauly." Teddy scrubbed his hands over his face. He felt sick. Dirty. Vile. "I don't fucking know."

"You have to tell her."

"Oh God." Teddy heaved, fighting but failing as memories of their love making and the condom breaking played on rotation in his brain. He stood up quickly, no longer able to control the vomit that had crept up his throat and he spewed it out violently as soon as he reached the toilet.

CHAPTER FIFTEEN

Fliss curled up into a tight ball, knowing the wallowing had to stop. Even Mrs. Rossington had sent her an email telling her off.

Fliss grinned, turned over and unlocked her phone to pull up the email her friend and confidante had sent her. She was to allow herself another week to 'weep herself silly' and then she must get back out there. Days were too precious to waste crying, especially over a man, Mrs. Rossington had written over a month ago.

Fliss stood up and looked in the mirror. She looked like crap. Her nails were chipped, she'd lost weight and her hair was stringy with grease. This was her last day of wallowing she swore, encouraged by the email.

She and Teddy were over. Done. He hadn't been in touch even though she'd waited two days for him to come and get her from Della's house. But his silence was notable. She'd bought herself a new train ticket and headed home in the clothes she'd borrowed from Della's stepdaughter Gabbs.

Ignoring the hollowness in her heart, Fliss went downstairs to check on her mother. They were alone and Fliss made sure the house was secure again before going over to the still form lying on the sofa snoring softly.

Fliss knelt on the floor and took her mother's hand. The brown skin, though soft, was paper thin and dull from years of needles and abuse. Fliss pressed a kiss into the palm.

She loved her mother, but this couldn't go on. She could not allow her mother to control their destiny any longer. If anything, being with Teddy had shown her how strong she really was.

***

"You need a night out."

"No I don't."

Fliss looked over at Mackenzie who was back at his old spot across the pod where it was easier for him to talk to all the new people on pod nine.

It was almost five in the morning, the third night of their rota and Fliss was feeling the effects of lack of sleep.

Her mother had gone through one of her episodes just after Fliss had drifted off to sleep and she'd woken to the sound of her mother laughing in that shrill flirtatious way that Fliss recognised as the older woman entertaining a man.

Her mother didn't go out any more, but delinquents remembered the availability of food, alcohol and even sex that her mother had once provided when the mood took her.

Going downstairs, Fliss prepared herself for the barrage of abuse she was going to get from her mother and the man. Luckily it was a local man Fliss recognised from the estate. He was a drunk and lived in government funded accommodation for alcoholics and was easy enough to deal with. Problem was, he'd brought along Pitface, the same man she had fought off when she'd been taking a shower. He scared her.

It wasn't until she'd threatened to call the police that they'd eventually left, but Pitface had glanced back, his thin lips twisting into a knowing smirk.

Her mother's rage had declined into a sniffle and Fliss calmed her even further by wrapping her arms around her thin body and rocking her like a child.

Fliss hadn't dared sleep once her mother had settled and was thankful when Eddy and TT had come back from their walk later that afternoon.

The snapping of fingers in her face nudged her out of her thoughts. "What?"

"I said you need a night out," Mackenzie repeated. "The whole man in London thing is over," Mackenzie refused to say Teddy's name due to his disappointment in him. "And I don't want you to revert back to how you were. You need a man."

Fliss arched a nicely shaped brow at him. "Are you trying to say I need a man to define me?" She challenged.

"I wouldn't dare," he slapped a hand against his heart. "I'm just saying you smile a lot more now and you've become dewy.

"Dewy?"

"Yeah," he winked, stretching his hands over his head as he spoke. "All soft and sweet like an over-ripe strawberry,"

Fliss laughed, she couldn't help herself. "The things you come out with. Dewy!"

"I know." Mackenzie turned to everyone. "Who's coming into town with us on Friday?" He invited. "Me and Fliss are going to get smashed," he explained. "And dance 'till morning."

"We'll go." Lucia spoke on behalf of Jarrett and herself.

"I'll go." This from the attractive new dark skinned girl on pod nine.

"Nice one." Pleased, Mackenzie touched his fist to hers. "Anyone else?" He asked again. "We'll meet at the Left Lion at nine. Go out for a nibble and then hit Hockley." He turned to Fliss. "You better be there," he warned. "Or I'll come get you."

"You don't even know where I live," Fliss answered, unimpressed.

"Yeah but I do." Priya joined.

"Fine. I'm not drinking," Fliss stated, "and I'm not staying out late."

"Fine." Mackenzie copied her tone then turned to Priya.

"You gonna come along?" Mackenzie asked quietly, knowing she would probably have to sneak out.

"If I can get out." She promised.

"Cool."

***

Fliss had had a busy but very productive day. Dr. Guresh was helping her find the right type of care for her mother. He'd been round and taken some blood samples from her and, depending on the outcome, they would take it from there. He also had a cousin who was a social worker and Fliss was going to meet her on Monday to see if there was somewhere private or government run that could look after her mother in a safe environment.

Fliss walked passed the statue of football legend Brian Clough and made her way to Market Square. She was actually looking forward to a night out. Mackenzie, Della and Mrs. Rossington all thought it a good idea for her to go out and enjoy herself. Mrs. Rossington even encouraged her to find herself a boyfriend for the night. Fliss laughed to herself. Mrs. Rossington was incorrigible.

Lucia and Jarrett, who were holding hands, and Priya were already at the meeting spot when she arrived.

"Look at you!" Jarrett said, once she joined them. "You look nice. Even heels."

"Thanks." Fliss smiled and looped her curls over her ears. She was wearing the cream bandage dress from that infamous night with Teddy and wanted to make fresh, new, happy memories by wearing it tonight. She figured it was a good plan. Why waste a good dress?

They were soon joined by Mackenzie, his close friend Marcin, whom Fliss had met before, the new girl and some other people MacKenzie had invited.

After a quick pizza dinner they walked around Hockley, going into pubs and clubs, swaying to the music or just talking. They finally settled into a more up-scale wine bar where the music was mellow and laughter and conversations flowed easily around them.

Fliss was enjoying herself. She had been overdue for a night out and was on her way to the bar to order a round of drinks when she saw him.

Those around her really did fade into the background and all she saw was him, as though someone had turned on a white spotlight. He looked torn and vulnerable standing there watching her.

Fliss didn't know who was more shocked.

"Crap." Mackenzie pulled her into the crook of his arm. "Smile Fliss," he whispered in her ear. "You can do one of two things, leave or go say hi."

"I'm going to talk to him," She replied confidently, although she could hear her own heartbeat thumping loudly.

"That's my girl. Show him what he's been missing!"

She walked towards Teddy and watched him take a breath and shift his stance as though he knew she could knock him off balance. Good!

Fliss watched as his eyes dropped to her body. Yes you ass-hole I still look good, she thought, and put an extra sway in her step. He wanted her. She could tell by the tell-tale glint in his blue eyes. Even from a distance she knew that heated look of his. It used to make her tingle all over. It still did.

But then his mouth tightened, his eyes dipped and when he looked at her again it was with revulsion. There was no other word for it and she stopped in her tracks, unable to move.

He hated her. He really hated her. But why look so ravaged? Had his mother told him things she didn't know about? He had said her background didn't matter. He'd said that he understood her. Why would he look at her with such distaste?

"Teddy?" For the first time Fliss noted the mixed raced girl standing beside him. She was tall, very pretty and she placed her hand on his arm. He looked down at her and tucked his own arm around her waist.

Now sick with nerves, Fliss forced herself to walk those last steps towards them.

"Teddy," she said, looking up at him.

"Felicity."

Look at me damn it, she willed.

He looked at her then, his brows dipping low as he shielded his blue gaze from her.

"This is Jess," he introduced.

Fliss held out her hand. She could do nice. "Pleased to meet you."

Her hand was taken in a quick reluctant clasp.

"You too," Jess replied automatically then turned to Teddy. "I'll just nip to the loo," she reached up on tiptoe and kissed his cheek.

"Be back soon."

Teddy watched her leave and Fliss thought about clearing her throat just to bring his blue gaze back to her.

"How've you been?" Teddy asked her with obvious reluctance a moment later.

"Fine." This was ridiculous, Fliss thought impatiently. Next they'd be talking about the bloody weather! "Can we meet for a coffee or something?"

"Why?"

"Because we have things to discuss."

His gaze flicked down her body, staying on her toned stomach longer than was considered polite.

"Are you pregnant?" He asked harshly.

Fliss gasped, remembering the last time they'd made love, the condom breaking and the huge argument that followed.

"No."

Fliss watched as his whole body relaxed and he tipped his head up as though to say thank you to The Man above.

"Then we have nothing to discuss."

Fliss had never heard him speak so dismissively.

"Bu—" she began again. She didn't want them to end the way they had. She wanted to tell him how grateful she was to him for being there for her. She wanted to tell him about her mother and all the help Dr. Guresh was doing with her. Teddy had started her on this journey and she wanted to share it with him.

Fliss reached out and stepped forward but he stepped back out of her reach and shook his head.

"Six." He stated tonelessly.

"What?"

"I'd asked Jess what her favourite number was between two and ten, she'd said six."

Fliss gasped and stumbled backwards into a group of men. She felt a pair of hands steady her, but she couldn't say thanks. The image of Teddy doing what he did to her with another woman was to unbearable to even think about. She felt her chest tighten as though someone was squashing her between two steel doors. She couldn't breathe and she put her hand to her throat as though trying to ease the pressure.

"Fliss I—" Teddy began taking a step towards her but Fliss turned and ran.

CHAPTER SIXTEEN

There were two police cars outside her house when Fliss eventually got home. She'd walked dejectedly around town for a while before finally flagging down a taxi.

Panicking and thinking this night couldn't get any worse, Fliss quickly walked up the short pathway and pushed open the door.

"What happened?" Fliss addressed Katie, an officer who had been to their home on several other occasions over the years.

"She's gone," TT said stepping forward wringing his hands.

"Gone?"

"That man from down at the rehab house came by," Eddy told her.

"Which man?" Fliss thought hoping against hope it wasn't who she thought it was.

"That young one with the crater face," TT described. "They took off just after you left. Eddy tried ringing ya, but ya phone is off." He explained.

Fliss pulled her phone out of her bag, remembering she'd turned it off earlier in the evening to save the battery as she'd forgotten to charge it.

"Pitface? She went out with Pitface?" Fliss asked with dread. "He's a drug pusher." She turned to Katie. "He'll have her shooting up tonight. Can you do anything?"

"She hasn't committed a crime, yet." The officer said gently. "We're only here because your friend flagged us down and I know how things are for you."

Fliss fought her fear. "But she's so vulnerable." She said, more to herself.

"Then she should have been somewhere safe being looked after by people who know what they are doing then shouldn't she?" The woman snapped but softened her voice seeing Felicity's tears. "We'll keep an eye out for her whilst we're on our rounds Felicity."

"Please, if anything happened to her..." Fliss begged, leaving the rest of the sentence unsaid.

The other officer who had been standing in the shadows came forward. "We'll see what we can do Felicity," he promised. "Pitface is known to us and he's got an ankle bracelet on," he advised gently, shooting a look to his colleague. "We should be able to find him."

"You need to do something Felicity," Katie said with grim truth. "You can't be here all the time and she needs proper care."

"I know." Felicity quickly explained her plans and the help she was getting.

After taking her mobile number, Katie gave her a hug and they left.

It was her fault, Fliss thought. The officer was right. She'd gone out leaving her mother with two old men who wouldn't have been able to stop her if she really wanted to go out.

"What are we gonna do Fliss?" TT asked, gently handing her a paper towel.

"I'm going to go look for her." Fliss wiped her eyes then blew her nose.

She ran upstairs and pulled out her black tracksuit bottoms from the back of her wardrobe and a thick black jumper, putting them on then taking off her jewellery, make-up and pulling her hair into a low ponytail. She needed to blend into the night, knowing she was about to put herself at risk.

"We'll come wid ya Flissy." TT told her as she came down the stairs.

The tightness in her chest hadn't eased and she put on an old jacket with a deep hood and wrapped a scarf around her neck, pulling it over her mouth so only her eyes could be seen.

"No, it's cold and late," she told them gently bending down to put on a pair of old trainers. "I know her old hangouts and I need you here if the police come back."

"You can't go out there by yourself, at least take Clyde with ya."

He opened the back door and the dog came bounding in wagging his tail from side to side and almost levitating when Eddy put the lead on him.

Eddy and TT had been in her life since Fliss could remember. The brothers had bought her her first two wheeled bicycle and showed her how to do a back flip. They were like family and, sniffing away her fear, she hugged them close.

***

Teddy waited. The meter was running but he didn't care. Something was wrong.

He'd followed, unseen, behind Fliss as she'd trailed around town before getting a taxi and going home.

Yes he felt guilty, but he'd had to stamp out that ray of hope he saw shining brightly in her eyes. They had no future.

Now he sat low in his seat as the two police cars drove away.

"We'll give it another ten minutes." Teddy told the driver.

"Sure, fine."

But as they were about to pull off Teddy watched the door open and Fliss, wearing all black with her hood pulled up and low over her face, walk out with the dog.

Teddy pulled out some notes, paid the driver and got out a few seconds after she'd passed the car and dodged into an alley.

He followed, hugging walls and fences, trying to blend into the shadows.

He wasn't dressed for a night of subterfuge, brown shiny brogues that slipped on the pavement, dress trousers and a white shirt that caught the slash of moonlight. His jacket matched his shoes.

Where was she going and why was she dressed like a gang member? He thought, as she quickly crossed the road, the dog straining on it's lead.

Teddy had never been this deep into the estate, being on the outskirts there was never any need and he had no idea where Fliss was going.

He had questions, but he couldn't get any answers from her directly. He needed to sever all ties, but that didn't mean he couldn't look out for her from afar. He owed her that much.

More twists and turns and he stood back to watch from a distance as she knocked on the door of a house so dilapidated it should be demolished.

It opened and Teddy could see a thickset man with a litre bottle of cider in his hand, wearing only jeans, talk to her and point down the road.

Fliss thanked him and moved off again.

At another house with grey metal covers on the windows to protect the glass from vandals, Teddy watched as again Fliss knocked and waited then was dragged inside with the dog.

"Christ!" Teddy sped across the street.

***

"What the hell?" Fliss demanded, as soon as she'd gotten over her fright and saw who it was. She didn't know him personally but had seen him around.

"How do we know you're not some cop or summat?"

"Do I look like some fucking cop? I'm looking for Pitface."

"Me too, he owes me money."

"He took my mother."

The man looked her over, flicked a glance at the group of men sitting on the floor behind him huddled over a small fire, before looking back at her.

"When you find him tell him Zero wants him."

"Zero?"

He put his hands on his hips. "You have a problem with my name?"

"It's very unique," she improvised instead of laughing like she had been about to. "If you see him first tell him Fliss is going to kill him."

"I know a place where he might go," Zero told her giving her the address and watching as she put it in her phone. "That Pitface is a filthy cunning bastard," Zero warned, opening the door to let her out. "Watch out he's bad news."

About to bang on the door himself, Teddy dived behind a car just as it opened.

***

Clyde kept looking behind him and whining. Fliss herself paused and looked back but didn't see anything so walked on, but listened past the early morning bird song for any other footsteps.

It was way past the witching hour, but it still felt creepy and Fliss sped up. She needed to get to Sandringham, an estate adjacent to this one, but still a good distance as the house she needed to go to was almost dead centre.

Dead Centre, what a phrase to use she thought, with grim humour. Clyde stopped and looked back again, his tail wagging slowly.

Fliss tried to drag him forward but he wasn't budging.

"What is it Clyde?" Fliss asked her dog crouching beside him and stroking his ears, as she peered into the distance. She couldn't see anything out of the ordinary. A row of wide, square terraced houses and unremarkable cars parked on the street. But from her vantage point she could see under the vehicles and saw the shoes and ankles of a person hiding between the cars!

A streak of alarm swept through her and without thinking, Fliss let Clyde off his lead.

The dog raced across the road going straight between the cars. She could hear his tail whacking excitedly as it hit the vehicles.

"Clyde!" Fliss shouted as loud as she dared this time of the morning. The last thing she needed was to bring attention to herself. "Clyde! Come here boy."

The dog ignored her.

She was in the middle of the road about to rescue her dog when the person stepped out.

"Teddy!" Fliss stood dumbfounded as her ex-boyfriend walked towards her, coming to a stop inches away. She'd never seen him look so angry. "What the hell do you think you're doing scaring me like that!"

"Why would you even let the dog go Felicity? He's your protection!" He blazed at her instead.

"Some protection," Fliss said noting the way Clyde was staring adoringly at Teddy. "What are you doing here?"

"Following you. What are *you* doing traipsing around the estate looking like a you're about to commit a robbery?"

"I'm looking for my mother." she grabbed the lead out of his hand and walked off. He could come if he wanted but she had to get to Sandringham. He fell into step beside her. "She went off with a junkie."

"I'm sorry," he answered. "When?"

"Whilst I was out enjoying my fucking self."

"Fliss don't." Teddy went to take her hand, but remembered. He shoved them in his pockets instead. "It wasn't your fault."

They crossed the road in silence, Fliss slightly ahead of him but Clyde kept baulking against his lead, the dog obviously wanted to walk with Teddy.

"Since when did you and Clyde become friends?" She asked, waiting for Teddy to catch up.

"When you were ill he led me to your bedroom," he revealed, taking the lead from her. "I never had a dog and me and Clyde here are great friends."

Why was he even talking about her dog? Fliss thought with annoyance. He should be explaining his presence!

Fliss glanced up at him, a million questions she wanted to ask on the tip of her tongue, but started with the most obvious one since he hadn't explained himself.

"What are you doing here Teddy?"

"I've been following you from the moment you ran out of the wine bar."

"Why?" She asked tiredly, realising too late she didn't want to have this conversation right now. She needed to focus. "Don't feel sorry for me Teddy I don't need it. Especially tonight."

Teddy didn't have anything to say. He felt compelled to look out for her. He always had. Simple.

Fliss looked at the address in her phone to double check the house number and stopped beside a house with a For Sale sign.

"You stay here," she ordered.

"I'm coming."

"They won't open the door if I have you with me."

She pulled off her jacket, unwound the scarf and took the tie out of her hair. She pushed the bundle into his chest where he grabbed them automatically.

"They grow weed in the attic and sell cocaine to their neighbours," she revealed plainly.

Teddy looked at the house. It looked like every other house on the street. A three bed semi with a patch of cut grass, neat borders and a silver people carrier on the drive. Everything about it screamed ordinary. No one would have suspected it being a drug den.

"Be careful," he warned but she'd already walked away.

Fliss knocked and waited and from the corner of her eye she counted two cameras trained on her.

A dark haired woman in her thirties, wearing jeans and a white T-shirt with a large pink sequinned heart on the front opened the door.

"Can I help you?" She asked, smiling as though opening the door to a stranger at five in the morning was a regular occurrence.

"I'm looking for someone and was told she might have come here."

"Can't help you love."

"Please, it's my mother." Fliss quickly showed her the photo of her mother on her phone. "This was taken a while ago and she looks a little different," Fliss explained.

"No." The woman took the phone from her. "No one like that came by tonight." She passed the phone back.

"How about Pitface?" Fliss begged. "She was with him."

The woman shook her head. "I'm sorry." She closed the door.

Fliss knocked again. But the porch light went off and the door remained closed.

Turning away, Fliss walked up the street to Teddy.

"No luck?" He asked.

"That woman was lying. She'd sold them drugs tonight I could tell."

"Where to next?"

The sun was coming up.

"That's it," she confirmed on the verge of tears. "There's no place else that I can think of but I'll ring Katie and tell her where I've been."

"Who's Katie?"

"One of the police officers that came over tonight."

They walked back in silence.

"Anything?" TT asked as soon as they got back.

She shook her head and walked over to her mother's sofa to curl up and hug the pillow to her chest.

"Don't worry Flissy. We'll go out again in the morning." Eddy told her then turned to look at Teddy.

"It's okay Eddy, he came with me," Fliss explained.

Both TT and Eddy looked at each other.

"We'll say good night then."

They went off to bed.

CHAPTER SEVENTEEN

"Do you want a cup of coffee or something?" Teddy asked Fliss, who was looking pale and fragile curled up in the chair.

"No, but help yourself."

"How are you feeling? Have you been taking your folic acid?" He asked, pulling a chair from the kitchen and turning to straddle it.

Fliss looked at the sofa and all the space that was there. Once upon a time he would have sat beside her and she would have laid her legs on top of his thighs.

"What's going on Teddy?" She ignored his questions. "Why are you here?" She had to know.

He shrugged, his brows furrowing into a deep V-shape.

"I needed to see you home."

"I'm a big girl, I've been taking care of myself well before you came," her pause was intentional. "And went from my life."

"You ran out of that club and I felt bad for saying what I said and followed you."

He still cared, Fliss thought. Deeply.

"So it's not true Jess isn't your girlfriend?" She couldn't help the thread of hope in her voice.

Teddy looked at the worn red and black swirly carpet. The confusion of the pattern soothed him.

"Jess is Jess."

"That's no answer," she pressed her fingers to her temples. She'd never played emotional games and wasn't about to start. Either they were in a relationship or they weren't. He didn't get to choose. "Look I'm tired and need a nap before I go back out there again."

"I don't want you going out alone."

She looked at him.

"As predictable as my next statement is going to be I really don't care what you want. Two months of silence from you then all of a sudden you're giving orders?"

"I stayed away for a reason," Teddy revealed with tight reluctance.

"What reason? No don't tell me." She made a huge circle with one arm. "All this! What? I'm not good enough for one of Iona's precious boys? Iona thinks you've come down in the world!"

"Felicity don't, you know I'm not a snob."

"Prove it." She moved to stand in front of him with her hands on her hips, forcing him to look at her. But he wouldn't meet her glare.

Turning her back on him Fliss whipped her jumper over her head before turning to face him in her bra. He'd been with her when they'd bought it in Portugal. A whisper of mocha lace and a band of matching satin. He'd spent most of that night loving her breasts through the lace.

"Prove it," she said again. "Tell me you still think of this."

Fliss heard his gasp with satisfaction but stepped back alarmed when suddenly the chair toppled over and he shrugged off his jacket and bundled her in it. With a hand to her chest he pushed her violently back into the chair.

Hurt and suddenly afraid of the tortured look in his eyes, Fliss buried her face in her mother's pillow and cried.

"I'm sorry," Teddy said harshly. "I'm sorry, I shouldn't be here," he admitted with a voice deeper than she had ever heard it.

There was something else going on here but she didn't know what. She looked around the room filled with too much furniture, too much stuff, yet it was different. The TV was off. It was never off. Fliss searched for the remote, finding it between the cushions and turned the TV on. She pressed the mute button before reluctantly looking at him again.

"I need you to leave and I need to find my mother. I don't know what else you have to tell me, I don't know why you have the need to protect me, but I can't do this. You need to leave Teddy."

"I can't."

Where those tears in his eyes? Fliss looked closer but he turned his head away.

"Then leave me alone Teddy," she breathed passionately, turning to deliberately sit in her mother's indention and hugging her pillow.

"I can't do that either," he replied honestly.

"I'm doing okay."

He smiled a small smile that touched her heart.

"I know you are and I'm happy for you, it's just that I always thought there was a future for us. Remember we made all those plans? Travel the world? Live in Portugal?"

She nodded, remembering their walk around the cobbled streets and making plans for all their tomorrows. It had been the first time she'd dare dream passed the here and now. He knew that.

"It's just that I can't be in a relationship like that with you any more."

"Why not?" She challenged, sitting up straighter and putting the pillow to one side. He was looking at her as though he was about to break her heart. But he'd already done that so what was left? "What did Iona say to you?" She whispered passed her throat clogged with emotion.

"She said,"

His look was tortuous, his soul wide open and vulnerable. Fliss knew what was coming was going to be bad.

"She sai—"

"For Gods sake Teddy spit it out!"

Teddy breathed in deep and moved to the front window. It was bright outside and he could hear cars.

He turned to face her, knowing what he was about to say was going to change her forever.

"She said we share the same father."

What he said was so ludicrous Fliss thought she'd misheard him.

"Is that a joke?"

"No joke."

"It's bloody ridiculous how can we be—" she couldn't even bring herself to say it. "It's just not possible. Your fucking white, as English as they come."

Teddy looked at her. He knew she was remembering the conversation they'd had in Portugal when he'd caught the sun and she'd said he could almost be classed as mixed race as his skin had deepened to a shade almost as golden as hers.

"You know your father. He lived with you," she challenged.

"I vaguely remember a man coming and going."

"Where is he now? He can confirm your mother is lying. God, Iona hates me so much she could lie like this?"

Fliss sat down again. Oh God, it was no wonder he was terrified she might have been pregnant.

"It's not true Teddy."

"She said it is."

"And you believe her?"

"She's my mother. Why would she lie?"

"I want proof. Pictures. A blood test."

Teddy remained silent. He'd thought of all the possibilities himself. He'd asked all the questions and grilled his mother before she'd left London. She'd told him she was seeing his father and that they'd had a falling out. That he had moved in with Felicity's mother for a couple of months, getting her pregnant. Then he'd left for Ireland and never returned to either of them.

"It's ridiculous," Fliss said again when he'd finished telling her all that Iona had said.

"What do you know about your father?" He asked.

"Not a lot, mum doesn't like talking about it and gets really upset so I've learned to leave it."

"Well now's your chance. We have a right to know."

"I don't want to know about him."

"We need to know Felicity."

"I loved you Teddy!" She cried suddenly. "I loved you like a woman loves her man!"

"Fliss don't," he begged.

"It can't be true Teddy."

He looked at her seeing all the emotions he himself had been through. The disbelief, the devastation, the grief. It was a death to who they were and what they'd meant to each other.

Now it all made sense Fliss thought, remembering the look of disgust on his face. It hadn't been directed at her, it had been at himself.

"You should have told me."

"You had other stuff going on in your life."

"You made me believe that I wasn't good enough for you."

"I'm sorry."

"I don't need your fucking sorry I need you to sort this out!" She slammed at him. "Find proof. Find your father, find mine, but don't you dare stand there and think that it's true because it's not! Iona is lying."

Teddy remained silent.

"She hates me, has always hated me and my mother."

"With cause Felicity." Why wasn't she getting it? "Think about it!"

"Why didn't your mother ever tell you?" She went on as though he hadn't spoken. "We lived a street apart. There was a chance we'd find out, become friends," Fliss asked him.

"We grew up being told never to play with you. You might not remember this but I remember playing at the corner, you came along, you must have been about three, maybe four. I remember sitting on the edge of the pavement showing you my marbles and my mother dragging me home. It was the first time she ever laid her hands on me."

Fliss started to laugh. It was just too funny. Her brother? He couldn't be. She had always been unlucky but this unlucky? Her laughter turned into gut wrenching sobs and she muffled the sound in the pillow.

"I can't deal with this right now." She went to wipe her eyes on her jumper but realised she was wearing his jacket instead. She felt sick. She'd tried to seduce him not half an hour ago. "I need you to leave. I need you to go back to London and leave me alone. I have to find my mother, she'll tell us the truth."

"Promise me you won't try and talk to Iona."

Teddy knew her, he knew how she thought.

"Why not? She tears down my world and I can't challenge it?"

"I'll deal with my mother," he warned. "And you deal with yours."

Her mother was gone, out there all alone and she had just found out the only other person she loved more than ever was her—she couldn't say it, it was just too weird. How could she be related to him?

"Promise me Felicity."

"Fine. I promise."

"I'll come back later and help look for her."

"I don't want you to come back. This is too much for me right now."

Teddy walked to the door leaving her with his jacket.

"I'm sorry Felicity."

"I'm sure you are."

He swung back not liking her tone. "What's that supposed to mean?"

"You got your out didn't you?" She accused bitterly.

"Explain?" Teddy walked back into the centre of the room.

"Our first stupid argument that night in London and this is our first conversation months later!"

Teddy pulled himself up to his full height.

"For your information," he began through clenched teeth. "My world was ripped apart that night!" He revealed. "You were spouting all that nonsense, ignoring me at the dinner, flirting with the twins and then my mother's great reveal!" He listed angrily throwing up his hands and swinging away.

"I was angry and I needed space to deal with it all." He turned back to her, pinning her in place with his scorching look. "Don't you get it Felicity? I wanted to keep you in my life for always."

Fliss gasped at the magnitude of his words.

"I'm sorry." She said in a small voice, totally shamed by her own selfishness.

He walked to the door, opened it, paused on the threshold but didn't look back before closing it behind him.

That was the last time Fliss had seen him.

**

Fliss went into crisis.

It wasn't surprising considering the amount of stress she'd been under. Her mother missing for a second day and the bombshell from Teddy had taken its toll.

Her body had practically seized up. The pain was so intense she called Dr. Guresh directly, who sent an ambulance for her.

On the third day of her mother's disappearance Officer Katie had called, then come to the hospital to tell Fliss the news directly.

CHAPTER EIGHTEEN

Two sentences on the news and that was it.

"A black female and white male were found dead in an empty house on the Sandringham Estate earlier today. Both thought to have overdosed, and now for the weather."

The news reader hadn't even paused, Fliss thought, remembering the pain of those words as she'd sat in a chair getting someone else's blood pumped into her veins.

They had been right there, right on that street, right beside the house with the For Sale sign! Fliss remembered in despair.

Fliss curled even further into the sofa.

She didn't deserve the right to call herself a daughter. A daughter looked after her mother. A daughter was supposed to be there, supporting and caring and encouraging. A daughter became the big sister when the mother couldn't cope. What had Fliss done? Failed in every way. She'd been right there.

The tears continued to fall, they'd been falling for days or maybe it was weeks? They'd been falling from the moment Katie had come to the hospital all those weeks ago, but whatever the date she didn't want the tears to ever stop. It was her punishment.

"Fliss, it's time honey."

Fliss looked up at Della dressed in black. Funeral day. There was to be a short service in their local church, a joke really as neither she nor her mother had ever set foot in the place, even though it was less than a two minute walk away.

Della held her hand and led her out of the house. Fliss watched as TT and Eddy locked the front door and the four of them walked to the church.

A handful of people were there sitting in the pews looking at her with pity. She didn't want anyone's pity. She was guilty, guilty of neglect.

A song, a biblical verse, another song and it was over. Nothing was said. Her mother had never chatted with the neighbours whilst hanging out the washing. She'd never given the postman a box of biscuits at Christmas. There was nothing polite anyone could ever say. You couldn't lie in church.

Faceless people walked out into the sunshine, pink and white blossoms bathed the pavement. Fliss saw it all, turned her back and walked away.

Fliss was sat on the floor, finally catching up on all the letters that had come over the past six weeks, when someone knocked on the door.

She'd changed the locks and tried to give Eddy and TT a key but they said they didn't need one any more.

Fliss smiled. If it hadn't been for the two old men, Della and even Mackenzie, she would have fallen apart. Hell, she almost did. Getting on a train the evening of the funeral and ending up in Skegness, where she booked herself into a B&B, texting Della that she was okay, then cried for three days straight.

Fliss looked through the peep hole and smiled.

"Hi, come on in."

"What are you doing Flissy?" TT asked, seeing all the boxes stacked against one wall.

"Sorting stuff out. Mum kept everything and wouldn't let me throw anything out.

TT looked at her with an odd expression in his soft grey eyes.

"What is it?" She asked catching his look.

"Your mother kept everything for a reason," he answered cryptically. "Let's have a cuppa."

"Okay," Fliss answered going into the kitchen. She'd already packed most things up. Mackenzie had a friend who was going to rent her a one bedroom flat in one of those new buildings that were popping up everywhere. Fliss couldn't wait to move.

"When are you back at work Flissy?"

"Next set of shifts next week." Fliss made his tea and handed it to him. "Tuesday night. Why?"

"Is there anything you want to ask me?" TT asked, sitting at the table.

Fliss sat across from him. The three of them had talked well into the night a few weeks ago where they told her about the children's home the three of them had been brought up in. They were the unwanted ones. Black and Irish. They became their own family.

Fliss didn't understand why her mother had kept it all a secret.

"No why?" She asked, stirring her tea.

"Your mother had a habit of stashing things away."

Fliss laughed looking around. "Obviously TT, look at the place!"

"No I mean like money. It's all over the house."

"She had no money."

"She had money."

"What are you saying?"

"Look at everything, read everything and throw nothing away unless you've ripped out the bottom and pulled out the drawers. Even the curtain poles. That was a favourite place."

He glanced at the narrow curtain pole over the kitchen sink stood up and, pulling his chair with him, positioned it by the sink and stood on it.

Fliss watched as he screwed off the decorative metal end, peered inside and, using a key from his bunch began to dig into the pole, pulling out a twenty pound note.

"See?"

Fliss looked at the note blankly.

TT pulled out another and another.

"All over the house?" She asked again in shock.

"All over the house," he confirmed, stepping down and handing her the money. "There are times when you will need privacy. This is one of them." He advised seriously.

Opening a drawer Fliss had already cleared, TT knocked the

bottom hard. It fell out and twenty pound notes fluttered to the floor. He twisted the draw for Fliss see the bottom she had wiped clean. "She lived here all her adult life Flissy, take your time and if you need help let us know."

He closed the front door behind him.

Fliss started in the bedrooms and found paper money of every denomination stashed in tight rolls behind pictures and mirrors. There was money stuffed inside the old fashioned headboards, inside mattresses, under false bottoms in the wardrobe and cupboard drawers. She even found money in the pockets of clothes her mother hadn't worn in thirty years.

Exhaustion finally made Fliss stop searching. It was two o'clock in the morning and she'd only done two rooms.

She had so many questions to ask. No wonder TT told her to do this alone! The pile of money on the landing floor was huge!

***

She took up TT's offer of help where they went through the rooms she'd already done and found more money. It became a treasure hunt and Fliss couldn't help getting excited about it.

They packed up and threw out as they went along. The furniture too old and worn would be given to charity. It took them four days to do the whole house. Only the sofa was left.

"We'll leave that for you to do by yourself Flissy," Eddy said. "That was her special place. God rest her soul."

They all looked at the sofa.

It all made sense to her now. Whenever Fliss was at work Eddy and TT stayed at the house. They'd known all along how much money was here. She felt her eyes prickle with tears.

"What am I going to do with the money? I can't go to the bank with it," she asked them. She could buy a small house and pay for it outright.

"We'll get it sorted." At the moment they were keeping it safe for her.

"I've got work tomorrow night." Fliss felt less and less like going to work.

"But Flissy, ya don't need to work or at least not yet. You have means now."

She looked at TT wide eyed. He was right.

After ordering a Chinese for them all they said their *good nights*, Fliss locked up behind them and sat on the floor across from the sofa.

So many memories in every curve of the cushions. Her mother's slight body making an indention that snuggled her close and made her feel secure. The dark stain Fliss knew was left by her mother's hair when she'd oiled it herself then went to sleep. Fliss felt the tears begin to fall. Blue and gold faded stripes that would have once been bright and regal brocade. That sofa represented her mother's whole life.

Fliss shuffled over to it and pulled off a cushion, remembering how her mother had become hysterical when Fliss had wanted to replace the sofa.

It was no wonder, Fliss thought as she unzipped it to reveal a square of yellow foam and tugged off the fabric. Predictably money fell out. Lots of old fifty pound notes. She repeated the process with the other cushions.

Then feeling around the inside edges pulled at the bottom frame. It lifted right out. Fliss moved the black plastic sheet aside and gasped.

More money, but also a treasure trove of her mother's life. Pictures of her mother laughing with two white boys who could only be Eddy and TT as they carried fishing poles with little red nets. More pictures of the three of them, school photos with her mother in a blue uniform and her hair in two huge bunches tied with red ribbons.

Fliss found costume jewellery and broken gold chains. A silver St. Christopher still in it's plastic holder and a crushed red rose. She put it to her nose, but it didn't have a scent.

There were vials upon vials containing little orange tablets. The labels dating back twenty years.

She found two old biscuit tins with letters and more photographs, but Fliss closed the lids to go through them later.

Moving to get a big box, Fliss transferred everything but the tablets into it until the bottom of the sofa was empty. Then she tipped the sofa over and seeing nothing, let it fall back.

That's it, she thought looking around the room. Everything but her own things and the sofa were now gone.

Tomorrow she would go to her sickle cell appointment, talk to Dr. Guresh about the pills and write her resignation.

***

Teddy hadn't even realised he was standing at the top of Felicity's street until he felt a young kid on a silver scooter slam into his legs, before riding off again.

It was cold, an unseasonal wetness bathed the street with dense misty rain. The kind that made you ill. Teddy had been visiting his family but the atmosphere was so strained, with his mother barely looking at him, he'd taken a walk.

There was a white panelled van parked in front of Felicity's house with its doors open. He could see boxes inside, some marked 'Fragile' others 'This way up'.

She was leaving? Where was she going? It had been weeks, but already she was moving on. He should be happy for her getting away from that house and moving on without him. He didn't think he could feel any worse, but he did.

Two men, Eddy and TT, came out carrying a large box between them with a black plastic bag on top. They stopped, put the bag with a pile of other rubbish bags by the gate, before walking to the van.

Teddy waited, feeling that familiar shard of pain pierce his heart whenever he thought of her. It was an old friend, welcomed. It reminded him that it was wrong to feel like this towards her.

He forced himself to move away but stopped when she stepped out wearing a short sleeved T-shirt and jeans, and talking on the phone. He wanted to tell her to put a coat on. Why did she never look after herself?

Her hair was piled on top of her head and he could see a streak of dirt on her cheek. When had he moved closer?

She saw him then and dropped her phone. He watched as her beautiful eyes dimmed and all colour left her face.

He wanted to go to her, wrap her in his arms, feel her body against his. No! He thought in distress. It was better this way.

She must have seen his anguish as her own pain mirrored his. Then as he watched she picked up her phone and walked towards him, stopping an arms length away. Her lovely eyes were huge, questioning and pleading.

She reached for him but he stepped back out of reach and shoved his hands in his pockets. He could feel a single raindrop drip down the back of this neck. With everything he had he turned and walked away, her wounded look forever imprinted on his heart.

CHAPTER NINETEEN

"I have an announcement to make." Fliss stood, having waited impatiently until the American rush hour had passed and they were able to talk without any interruptions.

"What now?" Ingrid said with a yawn. "The drama from your life lately is better than—"

"Shut up Ingrid," Lucia scolded, bending to take a ball of wool from her bag on the floor so that she could work on her latest design project. "She just lost her mother."

"Sorry I didn't mean it like that Fliss," Ingrid apologised.

"It's okay Ingrid," Fliss smiled gently at the older woman.

There once was a time when Ingrid irritated the living daylights out of her, now she just felt sorry for the poor woman. Stuck in what she herself said was a loveless marriage, looking after a man with four kids, non of which were her own.

"I've handed in my resignation," Fliss announced.

"You what!" Lucia exclaimed, sounding very British. "When did you hand it in?"

"When I came back yesterday," Fliss told her, reliving the feeling of excitement as she handed her letter to Monica-Louise. "I'm officially working my notice."

"Two weeks?" Jarrett asked.

"Works out at about three lots of shifts and then I'm done," Fliss explained, unable to keep from smiling.

"I'm gonna miss you Felicity," Jarrett said, pulling off his headset and walking around the pod to give her a hug. "It's not going to be the same without you."

"Damn right," chimed in Mackenzie. Felicity had already told him her plans several days before. "We've got to have a night out."

"Yeah!" Lucia agreed. "Go out for a meal somewhere swanky, not one of those buffet places. I don't do buffet's."

"Why not?"

"I had the prawns and threw up the whole night!"

"Everyone knows you stay away from the seafood at the buffet table." Mackenzie stated, without sympathy, shaking his head.

"It was five ninety nine a head!" Lucia exclaimed, planting her hands on her hips.

"Exactly," Mackenzie drawled, raising a single blond eyebrow. "How about a sit down meal somewhere?"

"Not too expensive," Jarrett said, walking back to his pod. "I'm a student."

"Me too."

"I'll foot the bill," said Monica-Louise, catching the latter part of their conversation as she walked over. "That's if..." she wavered when everyone gaped at her.

"Hey thanks for that," Fliss said quickly covering the silence that greeted her announcement.

The two of them had reached a new understanding since the conversation about her sales a few months back. Monica-Louise barked, and barked loudly, but she was fair. That's all Fliss wanted. Fairness and respect. Monica-Louise had been giving her doses of both and had been very understanding and compassionate throughout her illness and bereavement.

"That's settled then," Mackenzie said, ignoring the look of regret between Jarrett and Lucia as they looked at each other. "I'll sort it out."

"What the hell was that?" Mackenzie said to Fliss as they sat down to have their dinner at five o'clock. They were the only ones in the lunch room.

"What?"

"Monica-Louise offering to pay for the night out?" He fluffed the rice in his Indian microwave dinner. "In all my years here she has never done that for anyone. Not even for Della when she left."

Fliss shrugged. "She's trying to be nicer, can't you tell?"

Although they were alone Mackenzie leaned closer. "Do you think it has something to so with Jarrett passing her over for Lucia?"

Fliss chuckled remembering how their floor captain used to manipulate any situation so she was alone with the handsome African student. "Probably."

The ate in silence for a moment, Fliss tucking into her tuna salad and Mackenzie his curry.

"When are you moving into the flat?"

"Something has come up," she hadn't told him about all the money and wasn't planning to. "But I'm thinking of moving in at the weekend."

"Need any help?"

"I've only got a couple of boxes," she revealed, "starting afresh and all that," she waved her plastic fork around. "Buying myself a brand new shiny apple and taking bigger bites."

Mackenzie looked at her quizzically. "Huh?"

"It's what my friend calls taking a bite of your apple," Fliss explained. "Oh never mind," she rolled her eyes at his blank look. "I'm starting over and looking after me first and foremost. I've never done me before."

"I got you." He finished his meal and went to the vending machine, leaning his hand on it as he made his choice. "Want anything?"

"No thanks." She watched as he bought two packets of crisps and a bar of chocolate. "You're going to eat all that?"

"Yep," he opened the packet of salt and vinegar crisps first. "What's going on with him from London?"

Fliss sighed, she hadn't heard from Teddy since that day she had seen him on her street, and now that things were settling she knew she would have to start digging deeper into Iona's ridiculous claims. But first she wanted to move house.

She had this almost urgent need to move out and start over. She'd only come back to work her notice because it was the right thing to do and they'd been so nice to her. Otherwise she'd have moved already.

"Nothing is going on with him down in London," she told him, hoping he didn't catch the false lightness in her voice. "That's over and I'm moving on."

"That's my girl. Anyone caught your eye?"

"Mack, it's not like I've been out and about trying to pull," she said, using that very *British* phrase.

"No time like the present. You can't be wasting all this new sexiness." He waved his hand up and down her body as though she were the main prize. "We'll go to Birmingham Friday night."

"So far?"

"You need a change of scenery," he declared. "Too many memories in Notts and we don't want to bump into him from London." He whispered, comically cupping his mouth with his hand.

Fliss laughed, putting on a brave face. She wished she could share what had really happened between her and Teddy but it was just so sordid and embarrassing, and if it were true? God, it didn't even bare thinking about.

"No we definitely don't want that." She laughed, covering the pain as a little piece of her heart fell off. "You're a good friend Mackenzie." She thumped his arm playfully, thinking she really did cherish his friendship. When had that happened?

"Hey!" She laughed as he wrapped his arm around her neck and pulled her into a tight hug to kiss her loudly on the cheek.

"And I love you too. You're my work wife."

***

"I've not had a call in over an hour," Lucia stated.

"Me neither," Mackenzie said, not opening his eyes or moving his head where he was resting it on the back of his chair.

"Are the phones down again?" Asked Priya, standing to look at everyone.

Jarrett looked over at Monica-Louise, for once though the floor captain wasn't peering at her monitors but talking to another floor captain over at pod two. He waved his arm to get her attention.

"We've not had any calls," Jarrett explained as she walked over in her *too-high-for-work* black patent heels.

"How long?" Monica-Louise asked, peering over his shoulder to look at the time on his phone.

"Maybe half hour or so." Mackenzie lied. He knew better than to bring it to her attention that they'd all been sitting there chatting away and not reporting the lack of calls for over an hour.

Monica-Louise looked at the other pods, noticing the scripted chatter going on as normal. "I'll see what's up."

"Yes you do that." Jarrett said coldly, glaring at her as she walked away.

"Jarrett, you don't have to be so mean to her," Lucia said with a gasp.

"Yes I do," he replied harshly. "You know what she did."

"What did she do?" Ingrid asked looking up from her phone where she was playing a game of solitaire.

"Nothing." Both Jarrett and Lucia answered at the same time.

"Fine, don't tell us then," Ingrid finished, going back to her game.

"You feeling okay Fliss?" Priya asked, noticing that Fliss was abnormally quiet.

"Just a little tired." Fliss was finding it easier to talk about her sickle cell now that she'd explained it to them all.

"One more night for this set of shifts and then you can rest properly."

"I'm counting the hours Priya," she revealed honestly, "believe me."

"Do you hurt or anything?"

She smiled at the girl she'd known since she was twelve, although never spoke to until they'd started working together as adults.

Priya was a complicated character, all sweetness and light, but Fliss was very much aware of a streak of vindictiveness that struck when you least expected it. Priya had fire.

"Nope, I'm fine," Fliss sighed then stood up to put one leg on the desk beside her, stretching it out. "Just need a good stretch."

"I'm bored," Lucia declared. "How come the other teams are

getting calls?"

"Different lines I guess," Ingrid said, putting her phone to one side and getting up.

"But I thought we were all on the same thing?"

"They get switched about, we're primarily on North America at this time of the night and they do East Asia."

"So how come they won the Christmas competition?" Lucia asked.

"Do you know how much money the Chinese spend in our country each year? It's obscene," Fliss told them all, warming to the subject. "They—"

"What are you going to do once you leave, Fliss?" Priya asked, swiftly changing the subject as she didn't want them to start talking politics this late into their shift, it took too much energy and it always became a heated debate.

"Rest," Fliss said. "It's been one helluva six months."

"I hear you," Lucia said wistfully. "I want to go back to Spain."

"Why don't you?" Fliss asked, before noticing the look the younger girl shot Jarrett. "Never mind," Fliss laughed. "Go to Nigeria."

The *tip tip* of her knitting needles clashing stopped. "You must be joking!" Lucia responded in horror. "Too violent."

Fliss sighed dramatically. "Seriously Lucia? We've already had this conversation, remember?"

"No."

"Yes you do, I said the government overdo the whole scaremongering thing trying to keep us all within Europe."

"Oh yeah," Lucia acknowledged. "I'll only go if I'm with someone who comes from there." She looked pointedly at Jarrett, who suddenly found something on his computer screen very interesting.

"I've called the telephone people and they're looking into it." Monica-Louise advised, walking over. "If you haven't had your dinner, or last breaks, take them now please," she told them before walking over to pod nine and speaking to the floor captain there.

"I'm not taking mine yet, it's too early," Mackenzie declared.

"But she says to take it now," Ingrid said.

"I really don't give a shit what she says. For years I've had my last break at half six. I'm not changing it."

"Look at you being all rebellious," Fliss joined.

"You taking yours now Fliss?" He asked. They always had their dinner and breaks together.

"No, but I've got nothing to lose Mack. You want a warning from her tonight? Won't it be your third?"

"Three strikes and I'm out." He linked his hands behind his head and leaned back in his chair with a contented smirk on his face.

Fliss gasped. "You want to leave?"

"You're leaving." He pointed out, looking straight at her.

"But you know why I'm going, why do you want to get fired?"

"I want to go travelling."

"And you can't get time off because?" Fliss scoffed.

"I can't get that much time off with all my warnings, hence I'm being a bad boy and giving them a reason to get rid of me."

"That's stupid!" Ingrid scolded. "You won't get a recommendation and in this climate you won't get another job without one."

"Ingrid, Ingrid, Ingrid," he shook his head. "For you and Priya this place is somewhere to go and escape. Jarrett and Lucia are students. Fliss is leaving and they never replaced Della. I'm stuck in a fucking rut and need to take a bite out of my apple." He winked at Fliss, who put her thumbs up and smiled at him.

"Well as long as you can afford it." Ingrid didn't take offence. It was her escape route and she was saving really hard and doing as much overtime as she could so that she could leave her husband.

***

Over an hour later they were still without calls. Monica-Louise wouldn't let them go home so most were surfing the net and Lucia was now making earrings out of red wool.

"Truth or truth," Mackenzie exclaimed loudly.

"Huh?" Jarrett asked.

"Lets play truth or truth. Everyone stand up."

"Seriously Mackenzie?" Fliss grumbled tiredly. It was a struggle staying awake at this hour without calls to keep them distracted and the hours were dragging.

"Yep. Everyone up. I'm too damn bored."

"You could go on your break," declared Fliss, tongue in cheek.

"Very funny." He threw a paper clip at her. "For that I'll start with you. Truth or truth?"

"Isn't it supposed to be truth or dare?"

"Too boring, running around the pod on a dare, attached to a headset, just isn't doing it for me." Mackenzie explained wriggling his blond eyebrows at her.

They went around the pod asking stupid outlandish questions and laughing until they came round to Fliss again.

"Truth or truth Fliss." Priya asked.

Fliss touched a finger to her bottom lip as she pretended to ponder Priya's question.

"Hmm truth."

"At school in year ten did you really start that fire?"

Everyone turned to look at Fliss in shock.

"Erm no. Who said that?"

"There was a rumour going around that you did."

"I did many things but destroying a school isn't one of them." Fliss stated flatly. How could Priya even ask her that!

"I've got one," Ingrid said to Jarrett. "Did you and Monica-Louise have sex in the loos?"

"No," Jarrett stated quickly. "Next."

"Fliss, did you set the fire alarm off that time?" Priya asked.

"No. Next." She copied Jarrett.

"But everyone said you did," Ingrid said.

"Everyone like who?"

"Everyone, and you were the only one not at the pod when it happened."

"I didn't set it off. I remember going to the toilet and hearing footsteps on the stairs. It could have been them. I can't believe you all thought it was me all this time."

"Yes well you used to be an angry cow back then," Ingrid concluded.

"Not that angry! I was stuck in the lift for Christ's sake." Fliss shuddered, remembering how frightened she'd been stuck in that dark, enclosed space, knowing the building was empty and no one coming to her rescue. She'd cried buckets before she was rescued by that fireman.

"I should be offended," Fliss went on.

"But you're not," Lucia sent her a wink before turning to Mackenzie. "Truth or truth?" Lucia asked him. "Are you gay?"

"No." He replied.

"Ever kissed a man?" She added quickly, sending him a curious look.

"Yes."

Everyone clapped.

"Jarrett are you a rich prince slumming it in Britain?"

"Yes," he said seriously, then burst out laughing at their looks. "Kidding!"

"Ingrid I have a question."

"Go on Priya."

"Are you cheating on your husband?"

"You can't ask her that!" Lucia exclaimed.

"The choice is hers if she wants to answer or not."

"To me cheating is a physical thing," Ingrid answered.

"That's ridiculous. You can cheat without sex. Having a conversation with another man that you wouldn't have with your husband is cheating."

"Not in my book," Ingrid went on stubbornly.

"I guess your book is very thick then isn't it?" Priya commented snidely.

"Meow! To Priya!" Mackenzie declared. "Oh crap, a call just came through." He sat down quickly.

They didn't talk amongst themselves again until they said their

133

goodbyes at the end of the shift.

CHAPTER TWENTY

Fliss had never felt so liberated, turning the key and opening the door to her own flat that morning, it was amazing.

She'd cleaned from top to bottom, windows, doors, the bath and the shower and mopped the wooden floors. Now it felt like hers.

Exhausted but happy, she lay on the floor and looked up at the circular pattens of artex on the ceiling.

She smelled of pine detergent and her hands were dry because she'd forgotten to buy rubber gloves, but she felt great, tired but great.

Just another two sets of shifts then she'd be free to do what she pleased.

Noticing a thin cobweb on the light fixture, Fliss armed herself with the feather duster and was about to stand on the chair she had just dragged beneath the light when the doorbell rang.

Not expecting anyone and looking down at herself in a white, now grimy, T-shirt and grey flannel sweat bottoms, she opened the door.

"Surprise!" Mackenzie stepped over the threshold and pushed a potted fern into her arms. "Flat warming."

Looking at the plant Fliss was about to close the door when she noticed Marcin standing in the hallway.

"Hey Marcin, come on in."

"Hello Felicity," he said in his heavily accented English as he walked through to the small lounge where Mackenzie was looking out of the window.

Fliss looked in the hallway again to make sure no one else was lurking about before closing it. As lovely as it was to see them, she really wanted to spend her first day alone. She'd planned to have a long bath with scented candles all around it and soak for days on end. She'd held onto that fantasy for years.

"Nice view," Mackenzie said turning back to the room. "We're not stopping long, just passing through," he explained. "We're heading out tonight. Want to come?" Mackenzie asked expectantly.

"Thanks Mack but no," she said, noticing how nicely dressed they both looked. "I have plans."

"Not him from London I hope." He frowned down at her and crossed his arms high over his chest.

"You can say his name you know, I'm not about to crumble to pieces," she told him, placing the potted plant on the small island that divided the kitchen from the living room space.

"No thanks. I don't need to remember it or remind you of it either, we're moving on remember?" Mackenzie walked around her small space as though he were a caged animal. "Marcin are you going to give her that present or do you want me to have it?" Mackenzie said, eyeing the elegantly wrapped box his friend was holding.

Fliss watched, fascinated, as a tinge of red touched Marcin's cheeks.

"Here," he all but shoved it at her. "Welcome to your new home." He said, looking at something by her feet.

"Thanks Marcin." The box was quite heavy. "Can I open it now?" He looked at her briefly. "Of course."

Fliss smiled, she liked Marcin. He had a quiet *oldy worldly* air about him and was incredibly shy around her. It was cute.

"Oh goodness. My first guests and I haven't even offered you a drink." She put the box carefully on the counter and turned to them.

"What have you got?" Mackenzie asked, walking around her and opening the fridge wide.

"Water or semi-skimmed?" She told him, knowing the shelves were bare aside from a bottle of milk. "I haven't been food shopping yet."

"We'll pass," Mackenzie answered for both of them shutting the fridge. "As I said we're about to go out."

"I'm sorry I'm really not prepared. I was cleaning up," she finished, looking at Marcin who was, for once, looking directly at her. He had the warmest brown eyes with flecks of deep gold in them, she noticed for the first time.

"Where's the bathroom Fliss?" Mackenzie asked.

"Just through there," Fliss pointed down the short hallway. "Second door on the right."

"Thanks."

There was an awkward silence when he'd gone. She'd met Marcin a number of times as he was a close friend of Mackenzie's, but they'd never really been alone together. He was okay she thought, very shy and nice to look at. He was tall and muscular with broad shoulders. His hair was dark blond with a slight wave and his complexion wasn't pale, more like the sun had brushed him ever so lightly in golden rays.

"Where are you from again Marcin?"

"Eastern Europe."

He'd pulled himself up as though expecting a joke at his expense, she noticed.

"I know that," she said lightly. "Which country?"

"Latvia."

She tried to remember something about his country.

"I don't know anything about Latvia, you'll have to tell me sometime."

"Tomorrow."

"What?"

"Tomorrow we can go for dinner and I'll tell you about Latvia."

"Oh," she didn't know what to say. "Okay, I guess."

He smiled at her then. A wide smile that made the crinkles at the corner of his eyes deepen.

"I'll pick you up at seven. Yes?"

How had this happened? Fliss thought frantically. She wasn't ready to date. She still closed her eyes at night and saw bright blue ones seducing her. But then again why the hell not? She was young, she was free and if she carried on thinking like this she was going to burst into song.

"Seven is good," she told him smiling gently.

"What's good?" Mackenzie said, coming from the bathroom.

"Felicity and I are going to dinner tomorrow."

"What? Am I not invited?"

"You can come—"

"No." Marcin interrupted.

"I'm busy anyway." Mackenzie hugged Fliss close. "See you soon my darling friend."

"Bye," she hugged him back, hard. "Thank you for everything." She sniffed, feeling the tears come to the surface.

Mackenzie had been such a help for her these past few weeks, helping her flat hunt and navigate the whole renting jungle when she wasn't emotionally ready to cope with it.

He rocked her in his embrace. "Think nothing of it," he kissed her hair. "Come on big guy," he said to Marcin. "Let's go."

Fliss sniffed again and looked at Marcin.

"Well erm…" Fliss stuck her hand out glimpsing her unpolished nails.

"See you tomorrow Felicity." He smiled gently, holding her hand in both of his before following his friend out of the door.

Fliss leaned against it. Wow, she thought. What was that?

Although it was a secure building, habits never died and she checked the locks and put on the chain TT and Eddy had installed for her earlier that day.

With another delicate sigh Fliss looked out, seeing the early evening light settling in over the narrow boats. She had an unobstructed view of the canal and had to walk passed the castle to get into town. *Hell of a commute* she thought, smiling to herself. She loved it. The flat was situated on the opposite side of town from where she used to live and she felt as though she was in another city.

Putting on the kettle to make herself a cup of tea, Fliss saw Marcin's gift. She picked it up and shook it gently. She was glad he wasn't here to see how slowly and how carefully she pulled the white ribbon, or how slowly and carefully she peeled the thick silver and gold wrapping paper off. She folded it neatly before going on to the box.

Teddy used to hate the way she unwrapped presents, saying she tested his patience. If he could see her now he'd probably grab the box and rip off the paper himself she thought, remembering the last time she'd unwrapped a gift with him. They'd ended up making love on the floor and laughing because the paper had stuck to her bum.

Now why did she have to go and ruin her good mood? She thought crossly, putting a teabag into a mug and stirring in a single teaspoon of sugar.

The wrapping paper covered a pretty, embossed white box that Fliss knew she was going to keep and she lifted the lid. Beneath a layer of white tissue paper was a heavy white ceramic picture frame, embossed with roses. It was beautiful.

Marcin had put a lot of thought into his gift, Fliss thought uneasily. There was a card but, aside from recognising her name, the rest was in what she assumed must be Latvian.

***

Her intercom rang and, after confirming it was Marcin, she buzzed him through and waited at the door for him. It was exactly seven o'clock.

Not knowing what to wear, she'd played it safe with high waisted skinny black jeans and a white silky shirt. She could dress it down with ballet flats or up by wearing heels. She kept her jewellery simple.

He stepped out of the lift wearing dark blue jeans and a burgundy T-shirt with the cuffs turned over. He was carrying a large basket.

"This is for you." He put the basket on the counter.

"Thank you Marcin," she said, peering passed the clear cellophane to see all the edible goodies inside. "And thank you for the picture frame it's very beautiful."

"You like it?"

"I love it. I'm going to put a picture of my mother in it."

"Mack said your mother isn't with us?"

The gentleness of his words brought tears to her eyes and she blinked them away. "She died quite recently. Almost three months ago."

"Ah it's still very fresh," he reached for her shoulder and squeezed it gently. "I'm sorry."

"Thank you." She turned to go. "I'm just going to put my shoes on." She called out, going into her bedroom. Flats, she decided, looking at her array of shoes. This time last year it was a choice between old trainers or new trainers.

When she came out Marcin was looking at the chair, still in the middle of the room where she had left it yesterday.

"Why is the chair here?" He asked, looking down at her with a puzzled frown.

Fliss laughed. She'd been walking around it all day. "I was going to dust the light," she explained looking up. "See," she pointed, "there's a tiny cobweb."

He chuckled as he looked at her, before going to the kitchen to get a paper towel, stretching up and flicking the cobweb away.

"No more cobweb." He grinned at her.

"No more cobweb." She repeated. "Come on, lets go before I make you flex some more muscles for me."

She gasped once she realised what she'd said, especially when he laughed.

CHAPTER TWENTY-ONE

It was time.

Fliss sank into the bath one last time, holding her nose and wetting her hair as the warm, rose scented water flowed over her, soothing her fading dreams.

This was the best thing about living alone she thought, opening her eyes under the water and making out the glow of the candles beside the bath. Being able to have a long bath with the door unlocked, candles and music playing softly, was sheer luxury.

She loved it.

Trying not to splash water onto the floor, Fliss got out and wrapped herself in a large towel.

Eddy and TT had driven her to an out of town furniture store and she'd gone wild. Never before having the privilege of spending like she had. When she'd asked them where the money had come from, they been honest about it not all being on the government books, but that it was earned legally through odd jobs and from their circus days.

Putting on a long T-shirt, she walked into the living room and looked at the box over in the corner, knowing what she might find was probably going to change the course of her life. She was probably going to cry, she was probably going to get angry, she was going to miss her mother all over again and she was probably going to come face to face with her history.

She poured herself a large glass of red wine, dragged the box to the centre of the room and tipped it on it's side.

She sat on the floor to lean against the sofa, taking a large gulp of wine before placing the glass on the floor on her other side.

She reached for one of the old biscuit tins and pulled off the lid.

There was picture after picture of Fliss as a chubby baby, a toddler with a blonde afro, and others where she must have been around seven or eight. She'd never seen pictures of herself like this before. She hadn't known they existed and she certainly didn't remember any being taken.

Aside from the baby photos she never smiled. Fliss wasn't surprised at how angry she looked in most of them. It was sad seeing herself and remembering the solitude, the name calling and the fights.

Putting the photos carefully to one side, she found her hospital bracelet from when she must have had her first sickle cell crisis. She found a yellow plastic hair barrette and a teething-ring of keys. There was a small blue silk purse that skimmed on the outskirts of her memory.

She put those into a pile beside the photos.

There were strange coins and Fliss peered at them. Jamaican and Swedish. Fliss put them in another small pile.

She found her birth certificate and smiled at the time. She'd been born at three o'clock in the morning. It was no wonder she was always up late at night and preferred the night shift!

A few more hair clips and pins and the tin was empty.

Sniffing, she reached for the second tin. This one was lighter and she shook it. Nothing rattled.

She sipped her wine then opened it.

Lots of pictures of her mother with TT and Eddy, all the way up to their teen years. Pictures of her mother and a white woman sitting on the infamous blue and gold sofa laughing. Her mother had an afro and the woman's black hair hung long and straight down to her waist. They were smoking. Fliss looked at her and felt a chill sweep across her warm skin.

Iona? It could only be Iona.

There were more pictures of her mother and Iona. They'd obviously been best friends.

Reaching for her glass, Fliss realised she'd finished the wine and went to get the bottle, pouring herself a large glass and taking the bottle with her, sitting on the floor again, carefully picking her way and settling herself between all the piles she'd made.

There was a photo of them with two other men, both white one with dark hair with wide sideburns and the other with long, blond, shaggy hair.

Fliss looked closely, trying to find some kind of resemblance with them. She looked like neither of them. She put the photo on the sofa behind her.

More pictures, then another with Iona wearing a white floppy hat in a bikini, her mother beside her with a headscarf and a turquoise beaded necklace wearing a white crocheted bikini. Her mother was sitting on the knee of the blond man and they were looking into each other's eyes. His hand was on the inside of her mother's thigh. Iona was scowling at something.

Fliss could only see the man's profile and there was no information on the back. Could this be him?

A few more photos of what must have been the same day, and a single photo of the blond man looking directly into the camera. His smile was her own.

CHAPTER TWENTY-TWO

"Come on, out with it." Fliss stood up and looked at everyone on the pod. All of them, even Jarrett, dipped their heads down low, avoiding her gaze. "What's going on?"

It was her last ever shift. She was so excited and couldn't wait for eight o'clock. But something was up, her team-mates kept looking at each other and she'd even caught them whispering when she'd come off her break. Something was amiss.

She'd been given the obligatory flowers, cards and presents yesterday. She'd been sent the 'Thank you for your service' e-mail from management and she'd sent off her witty goodbye e-mail to her team-mates earlier in the shift. But something was off with them all.

"I'll say it," Mackenzie sighed, dramatically put his elbows on the partitions on either side of him, then looked at her. "It was my idea."

"What?" Fliss folded her arms across her chest and waited.

"Remember when we went down to London last year?" He began slowly.

"Yeah,"

"and you sang on stage?"

Where was he going with this? "Yes," she answered slowly, her eyes narrowing suspiciously.

"Well I thought it would be a great idea to enter you in a competition, and guess what?" He didn't wait for her to answer. "You're going up to Leeds to audition for *Time of Your Life*." He rushed clapping his hands.

"Ha ha very funny," Fliss stated adjusting her headset and moving to sit on the desk with her back to him.

"It's true Fliss," Priya told her. "I filled out the form with him."

"But why?"

"Because you have an amazing voice and you need to share it."

"I have no aspirations to sing in public Priya," she told her firmly. "Ever."

"Sorry sweetie, but there's something else," Mackenzie moved back and pushed the sleeves up on his shirt.

"What?"

"We collected all this money and made a bet with this bookie bloke I know." He put his hands up as though warding of a barrage of abuse from her.

"For?" Fliss asked calmly.

"You going and," he paused, looking at the others for help. "If you get the sound leveller to reach red we all win five grand."

Fliss started to laugh, it was so funny.

"Are you guys winding me up on my last night?"

"We're deadly serious Fliss," Mackenzie said, all traces of humour gone.

Mackenzie actually looked deadly serious, Fliss thought.

"We all put between two hundred and five hundred on you. You have to do it."

"On me?" She frowned, looking at them all, trying to understand. "As in a bet?"

"Because we love you and know you wanted to do that other show last year but were too scared," Mackenzie explained.

"Where did you ever get that idea?"

"From you, you watched it in the lunch room once and said, and I quote 'I can sing better than her and she just won.' I distinctly remember you saying that Fliss."

"I can't believe one little sentence a year ago and you go and do this. What were you thinking?"

"That you'll be forever grateful?"

"Don't be cute." She scolded her friend. "I'm not happy with you right now. Does Marcin know about this?"

"No," Mackenzie answered quickly. "Will you do it?"

"I don't believe this," she said once more to herself.

"Fliss, I used the last of my student loan on this," Jarrett told her quietly.

She gasped.

"Me too," Priya told her.

"Why would you do that?" Fliss asked, sitting down then standing up again. "I don't even know what to sing? Am I supposed to have one song or three?"

Mackenzie laughed, picked up his man-bag from the floor and pulled out a blue folder. "I've got the rules here." He waved the folder at her.

"And I made a copy!" Ingrid chimed.

"You've got this all figured out haven't you?" She asked them all.

They were all grinning.

"You'll do it?" Priya asked.

"Only because I can't let you lose any money on a bet like that. Jarrett and Lucia, don't do anything so stupid again," she scolded them. "And I'm going to need help."

"That's okay. You'll need two songs," Mackenzie said, leafing through the folder. "How about…"

And that's how her final shift ended with them all singing and sampling songs.

CHAPTER TWENTY-THREE

If u don't reply 2 this text within the hour. I'm going 2 yur mother.

Fliss slung her phone down on the table. She'd been trying to get hold of Teddy for the past week. He could ignore her as much as he wanted, but it ended now! She flopped into the chair in frustration.

She needed answers. He needed answers. They deserved answers. What was wrong with him anyway? She thought again. So okay he had moved on, but that didn't mean she could simply accept the words of his mother and carry on with her life as though it hadn't been completely derailed.

She'd shown the photographs to TT and Eddy, but they'd been touring across Europe for most of their teen years, so didn't know the men in the photographs. They'd only come back when Fliss had been born, and stayed when her mother began to unravel.

'Unravel', that's what they called it. Dr. Guresh had said her mother had been bi-polar. He'd found her medical records, confirming she had been diagnosed shortly after Fliss had been born. He also told her that her mother was drug free when he'd taken that blood sample.

The two swift beeps informing her of the arrival of a text interrupted Fliss's thoughts and she reached for her phone.

I'll be there tomorrow.

Damn right, Fliss thought, texting her address and waiting for some form of thanks from Teddy, but her phone remained silent.

She could just picture him now, locking up the pub and walking home after stopping off for his chip shop fix.

They'd done it many times together, she thought sadly and, not wanting to cry, turned on her laptop to e-mail Mrs. Rossington.

She hadn't told her friend the whole truth about Teddy, and Mrs. Rossington was quite happily encouraging her to move on. To appease her old friend, Fliss had told her about her little date with Marcin and how nice he was. Mrs. Rossington had e-mailed straight back to ask how he was in bed. Fliss had given her a detailed account of her date and what he looked like instead.

Their e-mails were getting very long and Fliss thought it might be nice if they talked on the phone now. Clearly the old lady was lonely and lived on the internet, as she would reply to an e-mail within minutes, Fliss now knew.

Her intercom rang startling her. It was almost two o'clock in the morning. Who could it be?

"Hello?"

"Buzz me up Felicity."

"Teddy?"

"Who else?"

Fliss leaned against the door. Teddy was here! She wasn't ready for this. The intercom beeped again. She could just picture his look of annoyance and she smiled. Teddy had no patience.

"What's name of my dog?" She asked, stalling.

"Clyde."

Fliss could hear the irritation in his voice. Good. She pressed the buzzer to let him into the building then opened her own door.

She should not be excited but she was. The last time she had seen him he'd dropped those ridiculous claims and walked out. He hadn't even sent a card when her mother died. He could have at least sent a bloody card!

Throwing back her shoulders, she heard the tell-tail ting from the elevator and the dull swish of the doors opening and there he was.

Dressed in blue jeans and a white collarless shirt, that was left loose, and tan loafers. His hair was longer than it usually was and looked damp.

"Is it raining?" She asked, as he walked passed her into the flat.

"No, I'd just got out of the shower when you texted me."

"Oh."

They stood looking at each other. God he looked good, Fliss thought feeling those things she always felt around him and crossed her arms over her chest, knowing her nipples were probably peaking through her vest.

She was dressed for bed; pink ribbed vest and pink paisley shorts. She'd been buying a lot of pink clothes lately and her hair was in a loose bun on top of her head. Teddy used to call her a light bulb when her hair was like that.

"Would you like a drink?" She asked, when he continued to stand there watching her. She'd never forgotten his long stares or how they used to make her feel as though she were the only woman in the universe. They still did it seemed. It wasn't right that he should look at her like this when they had a whole mess that needed to be sorted out.

"What have you got?"

She walked to her tiny kitchen, aware that he tracked her every move.

"Fizzy drinks, squash," she turned to him. "Milk?" She'd hoped to tease a smile out of him but he just looked at her, his blue eyes giving nothing away. "Erm, I've got beer if you want one?"

"Water."

"Please."

"Water please."

She let the tap run for a few seconds before filling a glass.

"That wasn't so hard was it Teddy?" She didn't wait for him to answer but moved passed him and sat down. "You said you were coming tomorrow," she reminded him.

He took a gulp of the water and put the glass on the counter, but kept hold of the glass as though afraid he didn't have control over his hands. "As I didn't stress a time I thought I'd come over now."

"What are you doing in Nottingham?"

"Sorting things out."

"Like?"

"Felicity, this isn't a social call. Tell me why you threatened to go to my mother."

"I don't normally take social calls at two in the morning," she pointed out tightly.

He walked to the window and turned the wand, opening the wooden slats on her blinds. He looked out for a moment before closing them again.

"I'm sorry. Let's start again," he began. "I'm sorry about your mother."

"Thank you."

"How have you been?"

"Exactly how you expect me to be. My mother died from a drug overdose in that same house where we stood in Sandringham."

"What do you mean?"

"Forget it Teddy," she got up and went to the white box the picture frame from Marcin had come in and lifted the lid. She took out the photographs and handed them to him before sitting down again. "You can sit down if you want," she offered, he looked at her but moved to the kitchen counter instead.

"That's my mother." He pointed out what she already knew.

"They were friends. Best friends it looks like."

He rubbed his eyes before looking at her. "Exactly."

"Exactly what?"

"They were friends and your mother stole her boyfriend."

"That's a lie!" Fliss stood up, walked over and snatched the photos from his hand, spreading them out on the counter. "Look?"

Teddy looked at them but shrugged.

"Is this your father?" She pointed to the dark-haired man that featured in a number of the pictures.

Teddy picked up the picture and stared at it.

"I don't know."

She picked up another one.

"I think this is my dad," she showed him the photo of the blond man with long shaggy hair. "I need you to take these to Iona."

He swung away from her then and ran his fingers through his hair.

"What would be the point?"

"The point being I need to know who these people are. Is this man my father? Is this man yours? Why did they end their friendship? We have a right to know!"

Teddy looked at the photographs again.

"Can I take these with me?"

"As long as I get them back."

"Of course," he said, stiffly picking them up and walking to the door but turned back. "How've you been Fliss?" He said softly.

Fliss leant against the counter, those four words spoken so gently touched her already broken heart.

"Fine."

"Are you still seeing Dr. Guresh?"

"Of course, he used to ask for you."

Teddy's lips tipped up into a small smile. "Nice bloke. You're looking well."

"Thank you." This was the conversation they should have had when he'd first walked in. They could be civil. "I resigned from work."

"Was that wise? I thought that maybe you'd cut your hours, not leave entirely,"

She shrugged, "It's not what I want to do."

"What do you want to do?"

He was supposed to know what she wanted. She'd once confided her dreams to him.

"I'm going to see the world."

They had planned their itinerary together. They were supposed to start in Portugal and drive through some European countries before cutting across to North Africa. It wasn't supposed to be like this.

The smile he tried failed. The look he sent her was honest, open and raw.

"Teddy?" She took a step towards him.

"Fliss don't," he said hoarsely.

"Please," she whispered. "Please," she walked towards him and wrapped her arms around his waist pressing her head against his chest. He felt so good, so solid and exciting. He smelt like freedom and dreams and when his arms pulled her closer she cried.

She couldn't help it. How could this happen?

Fliss could feel his whole body relax as though holding her was what he'd needed but then he took a deep breath and moved his hands to her shoulders to hold her at arms length.

She couldn't see through her tears. Cupping her face and using his thumbs like he did all those months ago he gently wiped away her tears before pressing his forehead to hers.

"I'm sorry," he whispered, stepping away to open the door and closing it softly behind him.

Fliss stood there a moment, trying to still her heart, then she ran to the window and opened the blinds. She watched as he left the building, his head bent low as he opened the outer gate then walked to his car parked on the street.

Briefly he was bathed in pale light but, instead of turning on the engine, he sat there with his hands on the steering wheel and Fliss gasped in dismay as he punched it several times.

With tears dripping, Fliss watched as he leaned his head against the steering wheel. She could feel his pain. Thinking he was unseen, he'd let his hurt show. She wanted to go to him, but knew that she couldn't. Right now their love was forbidden and she didn't have the strength to deny herself his touch. If he gave it she would take it and neither of them could let that happen.

Maybe he felt her eyes on him as he looked up suddenly, Fliss lifted her hand and pressed it against the cool glass.

His head dipped, acknowledging her wave, before starting his car and driving away.

Fliss stayed at the window watching his red tail lights until they disappeared.

Y do u have beer?

The message came through an hour later. Fliss was tucked up in bed going through her social media. She hardly ever commented or posted anything on her own wall but she liked to look and see what everyone else was doing.

She slid her laptop over to the bed and sat up. He wants to know why I have beer? She grinned.

Y?

Bcuz u shud not be drinking

Really? He was fishing, she thought, catching her lip between her teeth as she typed a reply.

Im not

Then y?

She smiled and snuggled into her pillows.

Friends cum ova

He made her wait a whole two minutes before he replied.

Gud 4 u

Good for me! She wanted to scream. But instead typed.

Yes it is. Gnite

When he didn't reply she texted.

I miss u

And hit reply before she could stop herself.

I miss u 2.x

Fliss drifted off to sleep with her phone in her hand and a smile on her face.

CHAPTER TWENTY-FOUR

Fliss bought herself a flirty new dress in deep red and a pair of gold strappy heels that cost more than she wanted to spend, but had fallen in love with.

It was the night Mackenzie had planned for her going away dinner.

Swanky was the word bandied about, hence the new dress and shoes. She knew she looked good. She'd gone to the hairdressers and had her hair flat ironed, her nails done and they'd talked her into having her eyebrows threaded. She felt girly and like the dress, flirty. She intended to have a good time tonight.

Fliss sprayed the last remaining drops of the perfume Teddy had given her last Christmas into the air and stood beneath the mist. Now she was ready.

Teddy, she thought, he was always there on the outskirts of her thoughts. She hadn't seen him since he'd come over, although he had texted and said his mother wasn't 'co-operating' and that he was working on it. What the hell did that mean? She'd sent him a text which he'd ignored. The infuriating man was so annoying she fumed, as she slipped on her heels, picked up her clutch and left her flat.

She was meeting them all at the restaurant. Who knew her work colleagues would mean so much to her after a year, she thought, as she got into the taxi. The ride took less than ten minutes but she'd timed it perfectly.

Jarrett, Lucia and Priya were already there, she noticed, spying them at the bar and walking over.

"Ready for a good night?" Priya asked, giving her a hug.

"Yep. How about you? How did you manage to get out?" Fliss asked, concerned for the other girl.

"Told them I was pulling another shift," Priya grinned. "I've been taking my clothes and jewellery to work all week she revealed.

Fliss knew Priya's brother went through her bag just to 'check.'

"You can stay at my house tonight," Fliss offered.

"Thanks, but I've made plans."

"Are you sure?"

"I'm sure."

"You've got my mobile number right?"

Priya gave her a hug. "I'm going to miss you Fliss."

"Aww don't," Fliss blinked hard several times. "You're going to make me cry and the night hasn't even started yet," she sniffed, hugging her friend back.

"Hey!" Jarrett interrupted, "Group hug," he commanded. "Come on."

They all hugged and then laughed.

They were soon joined by the others and were led to a long table that stretched from one wall almost to the other.

Fliss was so moved to see not only all on pod eight, but other members of the night team too.

It was a great meal, with lots of laughing and toasting and accounting of memorable moments with Fliss, she cried especially when Monica-Louise made a little speech, followed by Mackenzie.

It was perfect.

Some people said their goodbyes after dinner as they wouldn't see her because of their shift patterns, but most stayed and went on to the club.

Mackenzie had promised a swanky night and he was delivering in spades. They were swept along a short red carpet in an exclusive club and escorted to the VIP section.

***

Fliss was having a good time, a half hour set of every kind of music ensured everyone's taste was accounted for and, because she liked all music, she stayed on the quirky, sunken dance floor for most of the night.

Looking up, she caught a gorgeous blond man looking down at her, his golden gaze smouldering over her and she waved, swung her hips to the music alongside Jarrett and Monica-Louise one more time, before excusing herself and going to him.

"Marcin," she smiled, standing on tip toe to give him a short hug. He was dressed all in black which set off his unusual skin tone.

"Felicity," He grinned down at her, keeping his arm around her waist. "You look fantastic yes?"

"I feel fantastic, yes," she teased. "What would you like to drink?"

"You want to buy me a drink?"

"Yes, why not?" She tipped her head back to look at him with a slight frown.

"I usually buy the drinks."

"Not this time big guy, come on." She took his hand and pulled him over to the bar. "What are you having?"

"Cranberry juice please."

"No alcohol?"

"I'm in training."

"Training? Training for what?"

"Ice Hockey."

"You're an Outlaw? You play for Nottingham?"

He smiled, nodding, as he accepted the drink and they moved to the seating area.

"You deliberately didn't tell me that!" She admonished, remembering their first date where he was supposed to tell her about Latvia but instead plied her with questions instead.

"I'll tell you all about it tomorrow at dinner."

"tomorrow huh?" She smiled, now on to his tactics.

He picked up her hand and brought it to rest on his thigh possessively. "Tomorrow."

Fliss had the time of her life. They danced and talked, and those of her colleagues that were getting a little too inebriated they put in taxi's until it was just the three of them left.

"Want something to eat Fliss?" Mackenzie asked, as they walked through town.

"No thanks. I'll just be heading home now. My feet hurt. Hey!" Fliss yelled, caught by surprise as Marcin picked her up. "What are you doing?"

"Saving your feet."

"Put me down Marcin," she turned to her friend when Marcin held her closer. "Mack, tell him!"

"Who am I to tell the man to put you down?" Mackenzie shrugged. "Anyone hungry?

"I'm not," Marcin looked down at Fliss, "Are you?"

She shook her head then buried it in his neck again, as she was so embarrassed.

"I'm going to get a kebab from this place."

"I'm going to go home," Fliss told them both.

"Stay here whilst I get us a taxi okay?" Marcin turned her so that she slid all the way down his body. It was a very intimate thing to do. Then, still holding her close, he caught her bottom lip between his in an unhurried kiss before turning away.

Fliss watched as he walked up the street.

"You like him Fliss?" Mackenzie asked, coming out of the shop with his kebab and taking a bite. Ketchup and mayonnaise squeezed out of the sides and Fliss watched, laughing, as Mackenzie licked it all up.

"He's a nice guy."

"He really likes you, he saw you walking in town one day and you just so happened to be meeting me," Mackenzie revealed. "He had me on the phone all night asking questions about you. I thought I was in school again."

Fliss laughed, flattered.

"He's a solid guy, just what you need to get over him from London," Mackenzie explained, taking another huge bite of his meaty sandwich. "I've know him since boarding school."

"You were in France weren't you?"

"Yeah, hated that place. Made sure I got kicked out the first year, but Marcin and I remained friends. He's coming back." Mackenzie noted.

"Night Fliss," Mackenzie called from the confines of the car as the taxi pulled up at her gate and she and Marcin got out.

"Night Mack and thanks again."

"No problem. Go on in so I can get my beauty sleep."

"I'll pick you up around three?" Marcin asked, holding her hand as he walked her to the outer gate.

"Three it is," she answered shyly.

He dipped his head and kissed her before opening the gate and pushing her through it with a small smile.

"See you later Felicity."

"See you later Marcin." She gave him a tiny wave and walked inside.

She had a lot to think about tonight.

CHAPTER TWENTY-FIVE

As instructed, Fliss waited until she saw the flash of headlights from Marcin's car then she locked up and went downstairs.

He'd rung last night and told her he'd be taking her out and she was to be ready at six that morning.

She'd been horrified and had her excuse ready but he rang to wake her up half an hour ago and told her to put on loose, comfy clothes.

So here she was, getting into his car in loose comfy clothes at six in the morning when she hadn't even worked the night shift.

"*Labrit*," he said happily, as she slid in beside him.

"Hmm?"

"*Labrit*, good morning in Latvian, you're not a morning person?"

"I am, but I usually have a hot chocolate before conversation Marcin, but *Labrit* to you too."

Marcin laughed and touched her thigh. "I like you Felicity you are very strange."

"And I like you Marcin, even though you got me out of bed. Where are we going?" She finally remembered to ask as they sped through the empty streets.

"We're here."

Here being the back entrance to the ice arena. He parked his car, opened her door for her then went to the boot.

"These are for you."

He handed her a bouquet of yellow roses.

Fliss couldn't help but remember the one other time she'd been given flowers.

"Thank you, they're very lovely. Are you going to practise?" She asked, as he placed the flowers on the back seat, locked the car then led her through several corridors she never knew existed, until they reached the public area.

"I've already been," he said. "No, we are going to skate," he announced.

"No way I can't swim!" She panicked, backing up and trying to pull out of his hand.

He laughed, and Fliss realised it was the very first time she had seen him laugh so openly. It was a deep, rich sound coming from deep in his chest. It was a beautiful sound and she wanted to make him laugh some more, she realised, looking at the merriment in his warm brown eyes. Something, she didn't know what, tumbled in her tummy.

"This water is frozen Felicity, you won't drown," he coaxed playfully, his mouth still twitching in amusement.

"I've never skated before in my life."

"Good. I will teach you."

"I don't have any skates."

"Look," he indicated the shelves upon shelves of boots lined up for hire.

"Oh."

He laughed again. "Come on. No one is here and you can drown to your heart's content."

She found her size and put the boots on, all the while watching as he quickly put on his own boots, then walked over to pull her up.

"Look ahead, don't look at your feet," he advised, walking backwards as he held both her hands.

"I'm sure you say that to all the girls." She murmured with a wink, liking the answering twinkle in his eye.

Marcin let her hands go and she picked her way forward.

He opened the door to the rink and held her hand as she stepped cautiously onto the ice and immediately pitched forward then backward before throwing herself at the barrier, clinging on for dear life.

"Hold on to me Felicity," he advised, prising her fingers from the side.

"No!"

"Come on, trust me."

She looked at him and cautiously turned to face him, one hand still holding onto the side before she put both her hands in his.

"Good girl. Okay?" He asked, as she steadied herself.

"I am you big oaf."

"Big oaf huh?"

She grinned at him. "You must be an oaf to make me do something like this."

He laughed. "Keep your knees nice and loose and let me pull you. Okay?"

"You won't make me fall?"

"I won't make you fall."

Fliss closed her eyes and stumbled against him.

"But you have to look where you're going," he told her with amusement.

"Scared."

He pulled her further out onto the ice. They had the entire place to themselves. It was magical, Fliss thought, as she looked around the huge rink wishing she could really skate.

"Marcin?"

"Yes?"

"I like this."

"I'm glad. Come, I teach you how to stop and then you can practise on your own. Ready?"

"Ready."

Over the next hour he patiently taught her the basics and she was able to stumble around the circumference once before he drew her into the centre and pulled her around in circles several times as though they were dancing.

It was the most perfect date.

***

He took her for breakfast and then he took her home.

"I'm just going to put these in water," she told him, going into her kitchen, putting the roses gently on the counter before searching for a pair of scissors. "Would you like a drink, tea? Water?"

"Thank you no," Marcin sat on the stool to watch her snip the ends off the stems.

"Eleven," she counted. "Eleven roses?"

"In Latvia we do not like even numbers."

"That's a strange custom, why not?"

He shrugged. "Even numbers are for people in mourning."

She moved around him and placed the vase of roses on the low table beside the floor to ceiling window.

"Tell me more about your country, your family, do you have any brothers or sisters?"

"A younger sister, she's an athlete." He told her with pride.

He spent all morning with her, telling her about the woods he used to play in, his friends, the boarding school his parents sent him too when he was getting out of hand, and then finally hockey.

He was so passionate about the game Fliss couldn't help but get caught up in his excitement.

"Do you have a girlfriend back home?" She asked eventually.

"I did," he admitted. "Agnese, she didn't want to come to England."

"How long were you going out?"

"Four years," he answered reluctantly.

"Four years!" She exclaimed. "Why didn't she want to come?"

He shrugged. "She doesn't speak good English and she has a large family she would miss."

"How long have you been in England?"

"Six weeks."

"Six weeks!"

He looked passed her and she saw his sigh.

"I'm sorry."

"She made her choice," he said directly, capturing her hand and pulling her around the counter into the V of his strong thighs. "Lucky for you."

"Lucky for me," Fliss repeated honestly after he had kissed her.

"Marcin?" She was still within the circle of his legs, his hands were folded at her back keeping her close.

"Hmm?"

"I really like you, but—"

"But?"

"What are we doing?"

"Doing?"

She leaned back to look at him directly.

"Yes, we keep kissing and we've been out together several times. What are we doing?"

"You are very direct Felicity."

"I have to be."

"I like you too, and I think we might be as you English say—"

"British say," she interrupted.

"British? English? What is the difference?"

"English is what white people are everyone else is British."

He looked confused for a moment.

"We are all human," he stated with a flip of his hand before sliding his hand beneath her baggy jumper at her back. "Where was I?"

"You said you like me too." She reminded him with a cheeky look.

"So lets go out, you and me. Exclusively."

"I've had a really tough year Marcin," she told him earnestly. "My mother's death and my illness. I wasn't really expecting you to come along."

He smiled gently. "And I'm new to this country and don't have many friends and didn't expect to meet someone like you so soon either. We'll take it slow."

"I've only ever had two boyfriends. The first one years ago for a couple of weeks and then Teddy."

"Ah yes Teddy, the man who broke your heart and made you cry."

"Mackenzie told you that?"

"Mackenzie told me about the man in London, Teddy yes?"

"Yes."

"Do you still have feelings for him?"

"We didn't end on good terms and we still have things to sort out."

"Do you still have feelings for him?" He asked again.

"Do you still have feelings for your girlfriend?" She countered.

"Always," he replied honestly.

"Same. We'll take it slow?"

"Okay."

CHAPTER TWENTY-SIX

"I need you to tell me who these people are?"

It was early morning and Teddy, not being able to sleep, was round at his mother's house.

"Morning son," Iona said, letting him in and walking to the kitchen to get the mug of coffee that was already there. "Want a coffee?" She offered.

"Mam, can you look at these please?" He put the pictures down beside her where she looked at the one on top before moving to busy herself at the sink.

"How've you been Teddy? I've not seen you in ages."

They'd barely been talking as she'd been doing a good job of avoiding him, making sure she was in London, or Ireland, any time he was in Nottingham and always rushing him off the phone.

"I'm fine. I'm thinking of selling the pub and moving on," he admitted. His life in London wasn't the same any more. He saw Felicity everywhere. She'd brought light and laughter into his life. He needed to make changes whilst he could.

"Moving to where?" Iona lit a cigarette and opened the back door, leaning on the frame as she blew the smoke outside.

"I thought you gave that up?" He asked instead.

"I did, but I've been a bit stressed out lately. Don't tell Deck, he doesn't like it."

Teddy looked at her nicely dressed in black trousers and silk red top. She was wearing make-up and her hair was done.

"Are you going out?" He asked, she was even wearing heels.

"No, Deck will be downstairs any minute now. Why?"

"You're all done up."

She shrugged. "I like to look nice for him." She pulled on the cigarette two more times before turning on the tap to put it out and then hiding the stub deep in the rubbish bin.

"It's not even eight o'clock?"

"So?"

She was glaring at him now and Teddy knew her well enough to know when to back off. He didn't come here to argue and certainly not over things that didn't matter to him.

"Will you look at these? Felicity found them," he explained.

"You're still seeing that tramp after what I told you?"

"I'm not seeing her. We just want to know the whole story."

"She's a conniving bitch like her mother. Could never leave anything or anyone alone."

"She's not a bitch," Teddy stamped on his rising temper. "We want to know who these men are in the pictures." He walked over to where she was standing and held the small bundle out to her.

She ignored his hand and filled the kettle instead.

"Why? Why are you doing this Teddy. Can't you see this is hurting me?"

"This isn't about you right now," he blurted out angrily.

Teddy watched as tears filled his mother's eyes and her bottom lip began to tremble. It was always like this. She'd revert to tears to get her own way. Being the only woman in a household of men meant she got away with it. Teddy could see the pattern, she'd been like this his entire life.

Well he wasn't her husband and he needed answers.

"I need to know if this man," he searched for the photograph and, finding it, lifted it close to her eyes. "Is my real dad."

"No."

"Just look at it properly?" He gritted, fighting the urge to punch the wall.

"It's not him Teddy. What? You're calling your mother a liar now? That girl is filling your head. She's bad news, you're becoming just like her. Trash! How dare you come into my house and accuse me of lying!"

The tears had dried up, he noticed.

"Mam please, it's important to me. You were all friends."

"I told you she stole him from me! I told you she is your sister and you're still sniffing around her like the dog you are! She give you some last night Teddy?" Iona asked, her mouth twisting into an ugly line. "I should call the police! Fucking your own sister, it's vile. You're disgusting. You aren't a son of mine."

"Iona!"

Both Teddy and Iona turned to see Deck in the hallway.

"Deck, baby," she flung herself at her husband and buried her face in his neck, crying hysterically. "He's accusing me of lying Deck."

"Dad, I just want her to tell me the truth."

Deck was stroking Iona's back but looking at him over her shoulder.

"Leave them there Teddy, I'll show her them when she's calmed down."

Teddy hesitated. He didn't have time to wait for his mother to calm down.

"I'll come back later."

Iona wailed louder and Teddy watched as Deck patted her back, as though soothing a small child. It was pathetic to watch.

His mother was manipulative, she'd get depressed and not be able to function. Deck would have to make dinner and clean the house whist she lay upstairs, in full make-up, reading a book. She could be 'depressed' for months at a time.

"No," Deck told him. "You go on home and I'll sort it out."

Teddy had no choice. He couldn't get anything out of Iona in this state.

He left the house hearing his mother wailing and carrying on. It was disgusting.

***

Cum 2 London

The text came a few weeks later, when Fliss was out walking Clyde with Marcin along the canal.

She stopped and looked at it. He had some nerve, she thought crossly, weeks of nothing and then a command like that. Not even a hello.

"What is it?" Marcin asked her.

"I've been summoned to London," she replied. Marcin already knew about Teddy from Mackenzie and she'd told him they still had a few things to sort out.

"Oh yeah," he smiled, stooping to catch her lips in a tender kiss.

Marcin was very tactile and affectionate, he kissed her and hugged her a lot and she'd never felt so cherished and loved in her life before.

"By Teddy," she told him, nervously biting the corner of her lip as she watched him closely.

The indulgent smile slipped off his face and his eyebrows dipped into a sharp V. "Why?"

"Remember I told you we had things to take care of?"

"Yes," Marcin was looking over her head and Fliss could see his jaw working.

"It's very important and to do with our families," she explained.

"Why can't he come here?"

"He has a pub to run."

"I'll come, and we'll make a weekend of it?" Marcin suggested.

She smiled and wrapped her arms around him, giving him a reassuring squeeze. "That's sweet, but your training has started."

"I'll make time."

"Don't be silly. I'll be back before you've even missed me." She squeezed him again and again until he looked down at her. "Okay?"

"It's not Okay," he glared at her for a second before softening his stance and tucking her head under his chin. "But I understand."

Spending every day together for almost a month meant she was comfortable with him, she went on tip toe to capture his bottom lip with her lips for a nibble.

"Thank you," She said. Marcin was so uncomplicated and gentle she really liked that about him. "I'll just text him back."

When?

She typed.

Nxt train

Was the swift reply.

Can't

Y not?

On a date

BREAK IT!

No enjoying myself

Fine. Take last train & stay over.

No. C u tomoz. Will take taxi 2 flat. Bye.

He didn't reply and Fliss put her phone back in her pocket.

"I'll take the first train in the morning," Fliss told Marcin as he opened his car door and Clyde jumped in. Pets weren't allowed in her building so Eddy and TT kept him, but she always took him for walks whenever she could. "And be back by five." She promised.

"Okay Felicity," Marcin said grimly. "I'll drop you off at the station."

***

It was a typical evening for the two of them and Fliss was very much aware of the tension in his shoulders. When she'd offered to rub them he'd said no. When she'd asked if he wanted to leave, he said no, dragged her to him and kissed her deeply before going for his evening run along the canal.

When he came back she had a snack, he had a shower and they fell asleep watching a film.

She didn't know who made the first move but they began kissing. He was so large and wide, Fliss had to move her head to the side just to breath, but he was tender and loving. Taking his time to love her body.

When he picked her up and moved them to the bedroom she didn't object. It was time.

She liked him. He was good to her. He was good for her. He was stable and supportive, without any drama, and most importantly his family was in Latvia.

It was the beeping of his phone alarm that stopped him from making love to her.

"I have to go," he sighed, his body rigid with sexual tension and covered in a light sweat.

Fliss was afraid to move. She knew he took her silence for regret.

"I'm sorry," he kissed her nose and hauled himself away from her, before moving around her bedroom in concentrated movements. He was already in training mode. "I'll make it up to you."

Then he was gone.

When he dropped her off later that morning he kissed her so thoroughly Fliss felt branded. It was a feeling she wasn't sure she liked.

CHAPTER TWENTY-SEVEN

The train journey was uneventful and Fliss gasped in dismay when she saw Teddy waiting for her at the 'usual spot' where they used to meet.

"I thought I told you I'd take a taxi," she said, as she reached him.

"I've never let you take a taxi to my home by yourself before, so why would you think today would be any different?" He challenged, matching her tone.

She didn't know why she felt so surly. She only knew she wanted this all to be over with so she could get on with her life like he had done. Without her.

She didn't bother to answer but led the way to the exit. It was a bit nippy and Fliss pulled her light scarf a little closer around her neck and closed her jacket, wishing she had worn a pair of trousers instead of a skirt and tights.

***

Fliss looked at the house the taxi had parked in front of in confusion.

"Have you moved?" She asked, looking at the elegant detached house on a very upmarket street.

"No. There's someone I would like you to meet." He paid the driver and held the door as she got out.

"Who?"

"You'll see."

They walked up the wide gravelled driveway. Baskets and pots of autumn blooms were placed decoratively around. She wasn't into cars, but the one on the drive looked sleek and expensive.

Fliss heard an elegant tinkle inside when Teddy rang the doorbell.

"Teddy!" A tall white-haired man who looked to be in his fifties greeted him then he turned to Fliss, looking at her with wide eyed curiosity. "Is this her?" He opened the door wider. "Come in, come in." He ushered them through to the lounge and turned to Fliss expectantly.

"Felicity, may I introduce you to Jorgen." Teddy said. "Jorgen, Felicity, your niece."

Fliss gaped at the old man, who laughed. He looked so happy as he came over and hugged her tight.

"Come along my dear," he encouraged, letting her go and guiding her to the sofa. "Would you like to pour?"

Pour what? Felicity thought, before seeing the teapot with a real woollen tea cosy. She'd never poured a pot of tea in her life and looked desperately at Teddy.

"I think she might be a bit overwhelmed Jorgen. Can I do the honours?" Teddy asked, rescuing Fliss from the task.

The man, Jorgen, sat across from her smiling, then he leaned forward. "My older brother Alrick was your father," he explained. "But he died on the slopes in Canada a few days after you were born."

"I'm sorry," she said automatically.

"No, I am only sorry he didn't know you. He would be so proud. You are very beautiful and have his eyes." He looked at Teddy. "I think I'd better start at the beginning."

For the next hour Fliss learnt that her father had been a famous champion skier. He'd jilted his fiancée, the daughter of a family friend and came to England where he had met her mother. He had been in love with her, Jorgen had explained, but he knew she would never be accepted, being black. He knew she wouldn't cope in Sweden and left, not ever knowing she was pregnant.

But the papers learnt of Felicity's birth and tracked him down. He was doing his final run and coming back to England when he died. The family hadn't known of your existence until a few days ago.

"But that doesn't make sense," Fliss questioned. "If he knew, why didn't you?"

"With families it's complicated," her uncle shook his head. "I was a young boy and only learned what I know by sitting on the stairs late at night and listening to the adults. They're all dead now.

When he died, I'm afraid so did the need to find you." He took a sip of the tea Teddy had poured for him.

"I thought it was a story until Teddy here found me and everything fell into place. Your name, Felicity Pecora. Felicity was my great grandmother and Pecora is derived from Pecoraro on the family crest from the Italian great grandfather. If anyone had bothered to look for you we would have found you easily enough."

Felicity's head was spinning. She had an uncle, her father was dead and she was part of a family that was so snobby they'd disowned her unseen.

"Tell me something? Do you have a blood disorder by the name of sickle—"

"Sickle cell," Fliss finished for him.

"Me too!"

And so they bonded over their disease.

They spent hours together, Fliss learning that she had an entire family in Sweden now wanting to meet her. Her Uncle Jorgen brought out the family albums and showed Teddy how to operate the projector and they watched all the family films.

She got to know her father through those films. Hearing his voice and the laugh that shook his whole body. He was so charismatic and charming it was no wonder that her mother had spiralled out of control when he left.

It was early afternoon before they said their goodbyes, Fliss promising to come back and see him in a few weeks, then they were going to go to Sweden.

"You're very quiet," Teddy said, as they made their way to his pub. He just needed to check on things he said, get them something to eat and then they would talk. He promised to have her at the station on time.

"I just learnt I have a family, it's a lot to take in." She rubbed her temples, feeling the throb of a headache starting.

Teddy gave his address and when she turned questioning eyes to him he gave her his keys. "You go ahead, get some rest and I'll catch up with you later."

"But I need to get back," she said through the blur in front of her eyes.

"You have plenty of time."

He shut the car door and waved her off.

***

Fliss woke to the sound of the door closing. She'd fallen asleep on the sofa at an odd angle, if the pain in her neck was any indication.

"What time is it?" She asked, rubbing her eyes. It was still bright outside but she needed to be getting back. Marcin was waiting for her.

Teddy gave her a strange look she didn't understand. "Just gone two."

Still time she thought, relaxing.

"Why didn't you use the bed?" Teddy asked, shrugging out of his jacket.

"Why do you think?"

"Come on now Fliss," he stepped towards her. "You practically lived here."

"Yes well," she began then shrugged. "I don't any more."

"Come here."

"What?"

"I want to show you something."

She moved towards him with a frown. "What?" She asked, but gasped as he caught her by the back of her neck, pulled her to him and kissed her.

Fliss moaned as he forced her lips apart and swept inside to dance and tease her tongue with his.

"Teddy no," Fliss whispered, turning her head. "Teddy stop!" She pushed away from him. "What are you doing?"

"I've waited six months to have you Felicity." He breathed desperately, nipping the delicate skin at her neck.

"But—"

"You're not my sister. Not even a fucking cousin ten times removed. Iona lied."

"But—"

"We'll talk about it later," he growled, catching her hand and pulling her to his bedroom and, with a well placed hand, he pushed her to the bed and covered her body with his. "Right now I need to be inside you."

She couldn't think. He didn't give her a chance to think as her top was undone, her bra was pulled off and before she knew it he was bathing her breasts in kisses, sucking her nipples deep into his mouth whilst his hand went beneath her skirt, quickly stripping off her tights to sweep his fingers inside her panties. She moaned and bucked against him.

"No Teddy I can't." She pushed at him but he rubbed his hand against her, dipping his finger inside. "No stop," she twisted her upper body and pulled herself away. "I'm seeing someone."

Teddy stared at her, his blue eyes dark with arousal, his nostrils flaring ever so slightly.

Fliss watched as he tried to calm himself by sucking in some much needed air.

"Who?"

"His name is Ma—"

"I don't want to know his name," He snarled, swinging away from her to stand beside the bed. "You couldn't wait could you?" He accused.

"I—"

"Six months of hell I've been through, Felicity, thinking the woman I loved could have been my sister. Sister! Can you even begin to imagine how it felt?"

"I know, it was the same for me," she fumbled with her clothes. Her tights were ruined so she left them off. How had it even gotten so far? She thought shamefully. She could see her panties on the floor by his feet.

"If it was the same for you how could you take up with someone else so soon?"

"You did."

"No Felicity I did not."

"Jess?"

"A friend."

"Yes well you had me believing you'd moved on. You gave me nothing to hold onto."

"I don't walk on fucking water Felicity!" He swore at her. "I had to wait."

Fliss had nothing to say to that. He hadn't given her anything. No promises. He'd just left her, left her when she'd needed him the most. Her mother had died!

"I had to start at the beginning," he explained, trying to rein in his temper. "Iona wouldn't help and almost destroyed the photographs." At Fliss's gasp he added. "I'd given her copies. The originals are safe."

"Thank you."

"I don't want your fucking thanks!" He dragged a hand through his hair. "I had to go to Ireland and work from there."

"Your father?"

"Alive and drinking himself to death and calling Iona every name under the sun. Names she deserves, incidentally."

"I'm sorry."

"You are the only innocent in all of this. Iona was in love with him."

"Who?"

"Alrick, your father," Teddy explained. "He had the money the good looks, but only eyes for your mother. Iona sabotaged their relationship, thinking he would go to her. He didn't. He left the country, your mother was pregnant, unwell, and the rest you can guess."

Fliss sat at the edge of the bed. It was over. The mystery was finished. Iona best placed as the wicked witch, the evil stepmother, the jealous friend, all rolled into one.

"I need to go." She searched for her shoes.

"You can't."

"Why not?"

"You've missed your train."

"But you said I had plenty of time."

"I lied."

Rushing for her bag, she found her phone. Seven missed calls from Marcin and it was gone five o'clock. She should have been in Nottingham already.

"I hate you right now Teddy," she told him, as she waited for Marcin to pick up her call.

"The feeling is mutual Felicity, believe me."

"Hi," she turned away from his narrow blue stare. "Marcin, I missed the train," She explained and listened as he spoke. "Okay."

Teddy listened as she gave his address.

"He's coming to get me," she said turning to him.

"Lucky you." He said, before sending her a filthy look and slamming out of the flat.

***

Fliss stayed on the sofa and waited. It would take Marcin at least three hours to get to her and she was hoping Teddy stayed away.

What had happened? If she had had any experience with men maybe this wouldn't have happened in the first place. She and Teddy were over. He'd just drifted off for months on end without saying anything to her, the odd text exchange didn't count and he'd only ever initiated one of those anyway.

He never said they were over. He just starting dating someone else.

She was happy now, Marcin was a wonderful man. So uncomplicated, what you saw was exactly what you got. A gentle giant who, granted didn't sweep her off her feet, but physically kept sweeping her off her feet. She liked him and would never intentionally hurt him.

Why had Teddy lied about the time? And why did he think he could just snap his fingers and think they'd have sex? Too much had happened in the six months they'd been apart. If he'd explained as things had gone on maybe it would have been different, but he'd waited weeks and weeks giving her nothing. Telling her nothing.

But more to the point, why hadn't she taken responsibility for herself and got herself to the train station on time? That was the ultimate question. She'd let herself and she'd let Marcin down. He deserved better.

She was hungry but there was nothing in Teddy's flat to eat and she thought about nipping to the shop, but didn't dare move in case Marcin got here faster than expected.

She was right. He phoned her from the car letting her know he was outside and with a last glance around, she shut the door behind her and left.

He was leaning against his car, in full running gear she noticed and she ran to him. He lifted her up and she buried her face in his thick neck. She'd never needed the reassurance of his touch as much as she did right now.

"Okay now?" He asked, swinging her around so her back was against the car and she wrapped her legs around his waist. His warm, large hands swept back and forth along the underside of her bare legs.

She blinked back the tears. "I'm sorry," she cried.

"Shh, is he there?" Marcin asked with a nod towards the building.

"No, he left right after I called you," She admitted not liking the aggressive glint in his eye. "Take me home Marcin, please." She asked, pulling him closer.

He walked her around the car, still wrapped around him and gently placed her inside, buckling her seat belt for her.

Neither of them saw Teddy standing across the street watching them.

They had just navigated out of London and were on the motorway heading north when Fliss began to tell him everything that had happened to her, including her mother's overdose and even Iona's lie.

She wanted him to know everything that had brought them to this moment.

CHAPTER TWENTY-EIGHT

Fliss was in her kitchen when her front door opened.

"I'm in the kitchen," she called out, opening the oven to check on their salmon.

"Do you always leave your door open like that?"

Fliss almost dropped the plate she'd been about to put their fish on.

"What are you doing here and how did you get in?" She asked him.

Unbelievably, Teddy was standing in the middle of her living-room as though he had every right to be there.

"Which question would you like me to answer first?"

"What are you doing here?"

"I came by to see how you are."

"Why?"

"I'm in Nottingham for Pauly's engagement party and thought I'd stop by."

"Thank you but that's completely unnecessary and completely inappropriate," Fliss glanced at the clock on the microwave. Marcin was about to come home from his run any second now. She'd actually thought it was him, hence the door being open.

"Inappropriate, how?" Teddy challenged, pushing his hands into the pockets of his jeans.

Fliss looked at him properly, it had been a month since she'd last seen him. His clothes, though very nice, didn't seem to fit him as they should. They sort of hung from his shoulders without any shape and his jeans looked a size too large. His cheek bones were sharper and his skin looked dull. He really didn't look too well.

"Are you feeling all right?"

"Just peachy," he said grimly, walking to the counter that separated them, taking a peach from the fruit bowl. He threw it up into the air before putting it in the bowl again.

He noticed the picture of her and Marcin beside the fruit bowl and picked it up.

"You look happy," he stated.

"I am."

"Does he treat you right?"

"Always."

He looked at her. "Are you sleeping with him?"

Fliss gasped. "What the hell kind of question is that!"

Teddy pushed his hands through his hair. "I don't know, I'm sorry, I should go."

"Yes you should."

He put the picture down gently, too gently, and looked at her again. Fliss had never seen that kind of naked vulnerability from him before.

"Teddy?" She reached out to touch his arm.

"Don't Fliss. I don't want your gentleness. I just..."

The door opened and Marcin walked in. His hair was more a dark brown as it was wet from sweat and flopping into his eyes, the smile that had been on his face dropped as he spotted Teddy, Fliss's guilty look and the obvious tension in the room.

"Marcin, this is..."

"I know, Teddy right?"

Fliss watched as he walked over to Teddy with his hand extended. For a wild moment she thought Marcin was going to hit him.

"That's right," Teddy shook the other man's hand.

Both men turned to look at Fliss, but she busied herself with the salmon; using large oven gloves to take it out of the oven and placing the hot dish on the rubber protector on the counter.

"You're a long way from London," Marcin said, breaking the silence as he walked over to Fliss and dropped a quick kiss on her lips, before moving behind her and opening the fridge door to take out a bottle of water.

"I'm here for my brother's engagement party and thought I'd stop by and see how Fliss is."

"She's great," Marcin wrapped his muscular arm around Fliss's stomach and pulled her into him. It was a possessive gesture and not lost on Teddy. "Aren't you babes?"

"Great," she was feeling anything but. Teddy had no right making her feel uncomfortable being in Marcin's arms, but she did.

"Tell Pauly and Becks congratulations on their engagement for me," She pulled away from Marcin. "I'll show you out."

She walked to the door, opened it and waited for Teddy to pass. "Bye Fliss."

Teddy stopped right in front of her and picked up one of her honey blonde curls and pulled it, smiling grimly as he watched it bounce back. The gesture was as intimate as a kiss and she pressed herself into the door frame in dismay, too afraid to look at Marcin.

"Goodbye Fliss." Teddy said again.

"He still wants you." Marcin said as soon as the door closed.

She was in no mood for this conversation. "You'll have to ask him that."

"It's pretty obvious," he stated, moving from the kitchen to stand at the window. Fliss knew he was watching Teddy leave. "Did you invite him?"

"Really Marcin, you can ask me that?"

"Really Felicity, I can ask you that!" He snapped the blinds closed and turned to her, his golden eyes blazing. "Why was he here?"

Fliss stepped back. She had never seen him so angry. "He said he wanted to see how I was," she stumbled.

"How did he get in?"

"I always leave the door open for you, he just walked in."

"Did he come on to you?" He asked, looking at her closely.

"No! Why would you say that?"

"Because you lied," He told her flatly. "In London when I picked you up you didn't have your tights on. When you left you were wearing tights. Grey ones."

"What?" She couldn't believe this. All this time he thought she'd had sex with Teddy.

"Did you fuck him in London?"

"Get out."

"You answer my question!" His accent was so thick Fliss had trouble following him, she'd never seen him lose his temper before.

"I want you to leave." She said quietly as she failed to stop the tears.

She watched as Marcin went to the sink, turned on a tap and splashed water on his face. He dried himself with a paper towel before turning to her.

"I'm sorry," he said.

"So am I."

"I'll stay at my place."

"Yes."

Fliss watched as he picked up his large kit bag he always left by the door.

"Answer me this," Marcin asked from the doorway. "Did you kiss him in London?"

Fliss closed her eyes as she remembered the way Teddy had tried to kiss her and his desperation as he tried to make her respond. No she hadn't kissed him.

When she opened her eyes again Marcin was gone.

To Mrs. Rossington,

Have you ever been in love with two men?

After years of not being in any relationship I find myself having to ask myself that and I really don't know what the answer is.

Remember Teddy? From London? He came to see me and I had all sorts of feelings for him and then Marcin came home, I guess he picked up on those feelings because after Teddy left, we had a huge fight and I asked him to leave.

Marcin is a good man Mrs. R. a decent man and I don't want to hurt him. I really don't know what to do.

I'm sorry for burdening you with my love life, but I know you have a wealth of experience when it comes to men and I'm just starting out.

Please help

Your friend
Felicity. X

Fliss checked her spelling, sent off the e-mail and waited. When there wasn't a reply after ten minutes Fliss took a shower, made herself a camomile tea, and waited. Still nothing.

It was still early by their standards, they were both night owls talking via social media or e-mails until the early hours of the morning.

Yawning, she turned off her laptop and went beneath the covers.

***

"Where the hell are you?" Mackenzie asked as soon as Fliss answered her phone.

"Walking Clyde. Why?"

"I'm outside your building."

"Cross the road, walk down the footpath and turn right, I'll be walking towards you," she instructed, turning around.

It was strange walking Clyde without Marcin, it was something they did as a couple. But for the past few days she'd been taking a taxi to pick up her dog and spending the afternoon walking him alone.

"Shouldn't you have a coat on or something?" Mackenzie asked her as he approached. "Brr," he rubbed his hands together, before giving her a kiss on the cheek.

"It's nice and bracing," she said, "it'll be winter in a couple of weeks and then you'll have something to complain about. Come on."

"You want me to walk?" He asked in horror, glancing around suspiciously at the water and the grass as though little monsters were going to come out and ambush him.

She laughed, hooking her arm around his and guiding him along the path.

"So are you going to tell me why Marcin came round to mine last night roaring drunk?"

"He was drunk?" Fliss pulled him to a stop. "But he's in training. He shouldn't be drinking."

"Exactly. He drove himself to mine and passed out before he could tell me anything."

Fliss closed her eyes and sighed deeply before opening them again. "We had a fight."

"What could be so bad that he would put himself and others at risk like that. Marcin is the most straight up guy I know."

Fliss told him what had happened.

"So now he thinks you slept with Teddy that day?"

"Yes."

"You need to put it right Felicity."

"I know, but he's dropping my calls."

"Have you been round?"

"No."

"Do you want to though?"

"What kind of question is that?"

"You don't seem to be trying very hard to make it right Fliss." Mackenzie pointed out. "You're my friend and he's my friend, he's hurting and you're outside in this bloody weather walking the dog."

Felicity dipped her head. He was right, she hadn't tried very hard to make it right. A phone call the day after the fight and maybe one other. That was it.

"Are you still in love with Teddy?"

"I don't know," she replied honestly.

"Then before you wreck Marcin's life, because I can tell you now that boy loves you, you'd better find out."

"You won't tell him?"

"If he asks I won't lie," Mackenzie said honestly. "As I said, he's my friend and you're my friend. I'll be honest with you both, but I won't take sides."

She took a deep breath and watched as Clyde tried to get onto a blue and yellow narrow boat. She pulled him back and smiled an apology to the two women sitting on camping chairs listening to the radio.

"I like Marcin a lot," she admitted.

"I know you do."

"He's what I need in my life."

"But?"

"And I like Teddy, I owe him big time."

"Like or love? Or do you feel indebted to him?" He challenged. "Because Fliss, you were softening even before he came along."

"Softening?"

"Yeah, let's face it you were a right bitch," he said. "Last year? No one could talk to you without getting a verbal rollicking," he reminded her. "But now we know you were in pain and just too stupid to do anything about it back then."

"Charming," she muttered without malice, knowing he was right.

They walked on in silence for a moment, watching as Clyde tried to get onto the boats. She shortened his lead.

"I do have feelings for him Mackenzie," she said into the silence. "Different to what I feel for Marcin." She tried to explain. It was true she had strong feelings for both men. "I feel safe with Marcin."

Mackenzie noted the dreamy look on her face, but decided not to point it out.

"Teddy? Well, Teddy, I can't explain it," she went on, looking out across the marina.

"You have a lot of stuff to sort out Fliss, but please, for our friendship don't string Marcin along if you know he's not what you want, he's too nice a guy," Mackenzie advised. "And besides, he stood up for me when we were fourteen and I didn't want to play tennis, I owe him."

Fliss laughed, when inside she was a tightly coiled mess.

"When did my life become so complicated Mack?"

"The day you washed the 'f' word from your mouth and put on lipstick," he answered candidly.

"I guess it was," she thought sadly. "C'mon, lets go back."

CHAPTER TWENTY-NINE

Fliss, not normally a coffee drinker, gulped down the last of her drink as she looked out of the window for the taxi.

Seeing it arrive, she grabbed her handbag from by the door and locked up.

It was early, a little after five in the morning but this was the only time she knew exactly where Marcin was going to be; training at the ice arena.

He'd been avoiding her. After her talk with Mackenzie she'd looked into her own behaviour and knew she hadn't been fair to him.

She hadn't tried very hard to prove her innocence and he was walking around thinking she had cheated on him. That wasn't right.

Did she love him? It was early days yet but she did care for him. Deeply.

He'd been dropping all of her calls, until eventually he'd turned off his phone completely. When she'd walked over to his flat, if he was there he wasn't letting her in.

So here she was, being driven through town, seeing the last of the clubbers vomiting in the street and girls walking barefoot carrying their shoes as they stumbled their way home.

Fliss instructed the driver to the players entrance, paid him and got out.

She'd dressed carefully. Just enough make-up to make her look fresh, a single brush of mascara, a little blusher and a soft pink lip gloss. Her hair was in a loose bun on top of her head and she wore the pair of studded earrings Marcin had bought her. A baggy navy jumper over a red long sleeved T-shirt, leggings and trainers and she was ready.

The only thing really missing was her confidence. But she planned to fake that. She needed to make this right.

Pushing through the double metal doors, she walked down the corridor passed the changing rooms and out into the rink.

They were all there chasing up and down the rink after that stupid little black puck. It was such a weird game. She walked around to a seat almost parallel to the centre line and three rows up.

She liked seeing him play, was very proud that he played so well, but it was the violence of the game she hated. The players were just so brutal. Her gentle giant became a monster on the ice.

When Marcin watched old games on the internet she had to look away, and this was the second time she'd ever been to the arena to watch him play. He said she distracted him and didn't want her here. She'd been okay with that.

Settling into her seat she tried to pick him out. They didn't have their names on their shirts, with it being a training session, so she searched until she spotted him. God she'd missed him, she thought watching as he dashed up and down the rink.

It wasn't long until she was pointed out to him by another team-mate. He glanced at her and then ignored her for an hour.

Feeling her confidence dive even more, she waited until the vendor people had refilled the machines then went and got herself a hot chocolate.

When she walked back he was standing in the rink watching her. To her horror, Fliss saw it happen in slow motion.

His team-mates, not expecting anyone to be stupid enough to be standing still, crashed into him at top speed. He went flying, his helmet flew off and he hit the ice hard, sliding across the rink to crash into the side barrier.

Fliss dropped her drink and, without thinking, ran onto the ice, slipping and sliding and scrambling on her knees to get to him.

"Marcin! Marcin!" She shouted above the roar of fear in her ears, he wasn't moving.

His team-mates were surrounding him and she pushed the giants away to grab his face.

190

"Are you all right?" She asked, gently patting his cheek. "Please please please be all right."

"Excuse me little lady," the doctor said, just as Marcin opened his brown eyes and shook his head. "You okay, anything hurt?" The medic asked, as Marcin made to sit up.

Marcin answered in Latvian.

"He says he's fine," the other Latvian player translated.

"Let's give him some room," the doctor said and then, looking at Felicity, added "and maybe a little privacy?"

The players backed up.

"Okay guys that's it for today," Coach said, looking at his watch. "Marcin get up," he ordered harshly. "Your poor little lady isn't dressed to be on the ice."

Marcin and Fliss looked at each other and she grabbed his face and kissed him until he pulled her on top of him and kissed her back.

Neither heard the chuckles from their audience as they skated away.

"You stupid man. Why were you just standing there like that?" She admonished gently.

"I thought you'd left."

"Getting up at four in the morning to ambush you," she paused to give him a kiss, "you think I'd give up after an hour because you were being an idiot?" She asked, touching his brow tenderly.

"I don't know."

"I didn't sleep with him and I didn't kiss him," she told him whilst she had his full attention. "I wouldn't do that to you and when you know me a little better you'd know I don't play games like that. I'm a *one at a time* kind of girl.

I had a headache and fell asleep, he lied about the time and tried to get me into bed."

Marcin growled.

"I said tried, okay?" With both hands on his face she forced him to look at her. "Okay Marcin?"

He closed his eyes a moment then smiled. Pulling her down to capture her lips again as she lay on top of him.

191

"Okay Felicity."

The lights on the rink turned off.

"Come on it's cold in here." She struggled off him and gasped as pain shot up her leg as she tried to stand.

"Did you hurt yourself?" He asked, as she grabbed his arm.

"I think I hurt my ankle."

"What were you thinking, coming onto the ice?"

"That my man was hurt?"

"Your man huh?" He smiled smugly.

Her smile turned into a grimace.

"Stay here, I'm going to get the doc before he leaves."

She watched Marcin skate across the rink and then walk quickly down to the players quarters to come back with the doctor.

"You broke it," the doctor said minutes later, running his hands along her right ankle.

Marcin swore and threw his gloves down angrily.

"I'm sorry," she said, trying to placate him through her own pain.

"Marcin, stop being an idiot and let's get her up. Go get some guys."

Marcin skated off again.

"I don't know if it matters but I have sickle cell."

The doctor looked at her.

"I was going to strap you up temporarily but it might be best to take you straight to the hospital. I don't know much about it."

"Okay."

"I've never seen someone move so fast across the ice like you. If only the players were that fast we'd be in the major leagues every year," he joked, as he gently felt the bones around her already swollen ankle.

Fliss knew that he was trying to distract her. She was cold, her bottom was numb and she just wanted to go home and curl up with Marcin.

***

Five burly hockey players stayed with her at the hospital. The once sleepy nurses somehow found the time to put on lipstick and comb their hair. Fliss would have laughed if she wasn't in so much pain.

An x-ray confirming the break, a cast put on, then three hours later she was finally home.

"Well we've had an eventful morning," she joked. "It's not even nine o'clock yet."

"Fliss don't, this is serious."

"No it's not."

"Painkillers?"

"No I'm fine."

"I'll make you some toast."

"Please."

"Butter, jam or honey?" He asked, taking out the toaster.

"Butter and honey," she replied. "Marcin? You do believe me don't you?"

He looked over his shoulder at her. So very serious, his brown eyes searching hers. "I wouldn't be here if I didn't."

"I didn't tell you about it because I didn't want to hurt you. We're still new."

"Tell me the truth always Felicity, always."

"I'm sorry, and I'm sorry I went on the ice like a mad woman."

"You are a mad woman aren't you?" He chuckled, walking loosely over to her.

She grinned. "Yes I am. Now can I have a cuddle, a hot chocolate, my toast and then my bed in that order please."

Marcin pulled her into his chest. "A very demanding mad woman."

"Yes I am."

CHAPTER THIRTY

"Ready for this?" Fliss turned to Marcin and asked.

They'd been invited to dinner at Della's new house now that the refurbishment had been finished, and this was the first time he would be meeting her friend.

"Is she going to bite me?"

"Don't be silly," she laughed.

"Ask me to sign her chest?"

"Eww," she used a crutch to hit him gently on the leg. "Make an offer like that and see if I don't hit you harder!"

They were laughing when the door opened.

Fliss had never seen Della looking so worried.

"What is it?" Fliss asked, alarmed.

"We have a situation." Della glanced at Marcin then back at her. "I'm so sorry, but Spencer didn't tell me what he did and now we have another guest."

"Who?"

Della flicked another glance at Marcin.

"Teddy."

"Teddy? As in my Teddy?" Fliss said.

"The same," Della confirmed. "I can ask him to leave."

"No no," Fliss said quickly. "It'll be fine."

"I'm sorry." Della stuck out her hand to Marcin as soon as she closed the door. "I'm Della,"

"Marcin," he answered, distractingly frowning down at Fliss who was biting the corner of her lip.

"Do you want to go?" he asked, and repeated his question when she didn't answer.

"No." She seemed to wage some sort of internal battle with herself then pulled herself up to smile brightly at him. "I wasn't prepared that's all," she admitted candidly. "Come on. Lets have some Caribbean food."

Fliss knew everyone in the room; Isaac, Della and Spencer's son and Gabbs, Della's step daughter. Spencer used to be their boss at QB and that's where he'd found Della when he'd come to visit one night. His long lost love from Jamaica was how he liked to explain it.

"What the hell happened to your leg!" Teddy roared as soon as he spotted Felicity.

"I..." Fliss floundered with embarrassment.

"She broke it sometime ago," Della answered into the silence left by his emotional outburst.

"How?" Teddy blazed at Fliss, leaving the fireplace to walk over to her.

Marcin moved in front of Fliss, folding his arms high on his chest and planting both legs wide apart. "You need to calm down," he stated quietly.

"You took her on the ice?" Teddy bellowed at him. "She has sickle cell for God's sake, she needs to be taken care of!"

"Teddy stop it," Fliss told him. "It has nothing to do with you."

"You should be taking better care of her!" Teddy roared at Marcin.

Taking exception to the abuse, Marcin stepped forward. They were toe to toe.

Fliss dropped a crutch and grabbed his arm. "Marcin no!" She shouted, panicking as she saw that fighting glint in his eye, as if he was about to fight an opponent.

"Teddy!" She managed to get between the two men, pressing herself into Marcin for balance as she addressed Teddy. "It has nothing to do with you but I had an accident."

"Come on Teddy," Gabbs suggested, as the two men faced off above Fliss's head. "You can help me dish up the rice and peas." She pulled him into the kitchen.

Dinner was a little quiet, but again it was Gabbs's precocious chatter that drew everyone out as well as her outrageous flirtation with Marcin, saying she wanted to be his groupie.

Everyone laughed, especially as she took loads of photos of the two of them for her Instagram.

As soon as dinner was over Teddy asked if he could speak to Fliss alone. When she declined, he thanked the hosts, made his excuses and left.

∗∗

They were both very quiet on the drive home. Tonight had been a strain and she felt horrible for exposing Marcin to Teddy's arrogance. She couldn't believe Teddy had gone off like that.

"My Teddy," Marcin said, breaking the silence.

"What?" Fliss turned to him in confusion as they drove down Huntingdon Street.

"When we got there tonight you referred to Teddy as my Teddy," Marcin said flatly.

"It's just a figure of speech," Fliss brushed off lightly, thankful he wasn't able to see the heat of embarrassment on her cheeks.

"I didn't like it."

"I'm sorry."

Fliss thought he was going to say more but he didn't. Instead he raved about her friends.

"I've never had home-cooked Jamaican food before, it was nice." He went on conversationally.

"It was. Look I have a headache, can we talk tomorrow?"

"If that is what you want."

His accent had thickened, Fliss noticed.

"It is."

They drove the rest of the way in silence. Marcin walked her to her door saw her inside and left after a polite kiss on the cheek.

196

CHAPTER THIRTY-ONE

He pressed the intercom.

"Did you forget something Marcin?"

He made a sound and quickly pulled the door open when it buzzed.

"What are you doing?" Fliss asked, backing up as far as she could in the room when she opened her door. "You behaved appallingly tonight, challenging Marcin like that! It was disgusting."

"I apologise," Teddy said quietly, closing the door behind him and moving to stand in the middle of the room.

He looked tortured Fliss thought, noticing the lines beside his mouth were deeper than usual and his mouth tight and grim. Fliss hardened her heart.

"You shouldn't be here."

"I know. We established that once before remember."

They looked at each other across the space, both of them remembering the one other time he had been inside her flat and the question he had asked.

"Your boyfriend seems decent," Teddy said unexpectedly.

"He is."

"Good to you?"

"Yes. Very. But as you rightly pointed out, we've already had this conversation."

"So we have."

"Stay where you are." Fliss put up a crutch to ward him off when he stepped closer.

"What are you going to do, stab me with it?" He challenged, stepping closer, then thinking better of it and sat in her single chair instead.

He scrubbed a hand over his face. "I'm sorry Felicity, my behaviour tonight was bad. I wasn't expecting you and then to see you hurt, and with him, kind of sent me over the edge," he revealed honestly.

He turned to look at her on the other side of the room, practically plastered against the wall as though he was carrying a disease.

"Please come and sit down." He indicated the sofa with a wave of his hand. "I just want to talk. How did you hurt yourself?"

"You shouldn't be here," she repeated as she stepped around him and sat awkwardly in the chair, placing the crutches beside her.

"I won't stay long."

"Marcin hurt himself and I ran onto the ice like an idiot and broke my ankle."

"That was a stupid thing to do."

"He was hurt."

Teddy looked at her, in other words she would do it again for the man she loved, Teddy interpreted.

"Pauly's having a Christmas wedding."

"That's nice."

"He intends to invite you."

"Marcin too?"

"I doubt it."

"Then I won't be going."

"I need to have sex with you."

"What?" Surely he hadn't said what she thought he had said. "What did you just say?"

"I said I need to sleep with you again."

"Get out." Fliss moved to pick up her crutches.

"Please listen to me Felicity." He moved forward so that their knees were almost touching. "Do you think this is easy for me?" He didn't wait for her to answer. "I've not been in a physical relationship since you."

"So?"

"Don't," he urged. "You're not a cruel person Fliss, don't try to be."

"You have no idea what kind of person I've become."

"I've been completely emasculated," he revealed flatly. "I've not been in a physical relationship because when I'm with a woman and we get to that stage all I can think about and all I can remember was that feeling of disgust."

Fliss gasped. "That's a horrible thing to say!"

"Not at you," he clarified quickly, standing up and walking to the counter. "At me! The feelings I had for you, even when I knew you could have been my sister. I can't get passed it." He ran his hands roughly through his hair before looking at her, his eyes dimming with anguish.

"That's not my problem Teddy,"

He came to her, went on his knees and grabbed her hands.

"One night is all I ask."

"Are you out of your mind?"

"One night. Fliss I'm begging you."

Fliss wrenched her hands away and leaned back as far as she could in her seat when he buried his head in her lap and wrapped his arms around her hips, hugging her close.

"I have a boyfriend. He's the loveliest person I know. Please get off me Teddy. It's not right."

"He won't find out," Teddy stressed urgently. "We'll go out of town. I need you to do this."

"No. Get off me Teddy. You're scaring me." It was true, he was. She knew he would never physically hurt her, but he was behaving like a different person. Desperate. She had never seen him like this.

He moved away and Fliss, ignoring her crutches, hopped to the counter.

"Every time I close my eyes I see you with him, making love with him knowing it should be me deep inside you. It's driving me insane!" He shouted in torment. "I'm stuck Felicity. Stuck!"

"Get out!" Fliss rifled through her handbag for her phone. "If you don't leave I'll call the police."

"You owe me."

They watched each other.

"Please consider it," he asked quietly as he moved to the door.

"Never. I'm with someone else now. I would never betray him like that."

She watched him walk to the door, closing it quietly behind him.

She held herself together as she prepared for bed. What had just happened, she thought, as she lay in the darkness. Why would he even think she would do such a thing and why was she even remembering the feel of him so close to her?

She folded her arms across her breasts to ease the pressure that had been there since he'd walked into the flat. He'd not even attempted to hide his own arousal, she remembered, as she moved her fingers to her inner thighs.

It was sexual. Nothing more. Sex alone couldn't sustain a relationship.

CHAPTER THIRTY-TWO

Fliss was still in bed using a ruler to try and reach an itch on her broken ankle when she made the call.

"Hi, morning," she said when he answered on the second ring.

"*Labrit*, Felicity."

"*Labrit,*" she repeated. "Did you have a good practise?"

"The usual. What's up?"

"Are you going to come over for breakfast?"

There was a pause.

Normally she didn't ask, he just came over right after his morning run.

It was way past that time. She put the ruler on her bedside table when he didn't answer straight away.

"Not today," he said eventually.

"Oh why not? No don't answer," she said more to herself. "Can I talk to you about something?"

"Do you need me to come over because I thought I'd take a nap."

This was not their routine. He took his naps on her sofa or her bed if she was out.

"The phone is okay." She took a breath. "I need to tell you something and I'm not sure how you're going to take it, but we tell the truth always, yes?" She finished in his accent. He didn't laugh.

"Yes."

"Teddy came by after you dropped me off last night," she told him in a rush.

"I know."

"You know?" She sat up in bed.

"I started driving off when I saw a man jump the gate. I got out and saw when he entered the building."

"Oh."

"I should be asking you why you let him in."

"Why aren't you?"

"Because you both obviously haven't ended things. You're still emotionally involved."

"I've ended it."

"Have you? Honestly?"

"He asked me to sleep with him."

"And you said?"

"Marcin, I'm with you, we've been over this."

"Yes we have. Look, practise was hard today, coach was extra tough so I really need to get some rest."

"Will you come by later?" She asked anxiously.

There was a long pause and she really thought he wasn't going to answer.

"In the afternoon, we can try that vegetarian restaurant Della told us about last night."

"I'd like that. Bye Marcin."

"*Uz redzesanos*." He hung up.

Fliss lay back in the bed and looked up at the ceiling. Marcin was mad. This was the first time he hadn't come over to her flat after practise.

He sounded, not abrupt she mused, more polite as though he was making arrangements with a stranger.

She would have preferred it if he'd shouted, maybe sworn, but not this. His response to having another man proposition his girlfriend? No reaction.

If she had been propositioned by another man while going out with Teddy he would have gone ballistic and probably smashed the guy's face in. She didn't condone violence, but God knew Marcin's reaction was giving her things to think about.

***

Fliss hung up the phone and looked out over at the marina.

Her new uncle, Jorgen, was putting pressure on her to go to Sweden with him. Now that she had finished work it would be the perfect opportunity she knew, but she would have to have a word with Marcin when he came home.

She smiled as, right on time, she watched him run the last few metres along the path, cross the road and jog the final steps to the gates. He was breathing hard.

They were getting closer and apart from his games and training sessions they did everything together. Her cast was due to come off in another few weeks and then she would be free to continue her lessons on the ice.

"Hi there," she said as he opened the door, all handsome in his sweatiness, she thought.

"*Labdien*," he said instead and waited with an eyebrow raised for her to reply in his language. He grinned when she did, even adding the additional phrase of 'how was your run?' To him.

"Good. What's up?" He asked.

He was very perceptive like that when it came to her feelings, she knew.

"Jorgen has called again. He wants me to go to Sweden. I can't keep putting him off."

"Go, it's not far," he said, as he unlaced his running shoes and walked back to the door to place them on the mat.

"What about you?"

"I have the games coming up," he shrugged. "And we don't want the air to be too cold for you as it might mess with your health."

"True." She hadn't thought about that.

"Go."

"If I didn't know any better I'd think you were getting rid of me," she joked.

He came over. "Never. It's only going to get busier for me and you need to meet your family. Family is important."

"Do you want to come?" She asked, not really relishing the thought of meeting strangers by herself.

He shook his head and dropped a quick kiss on her nose. "Not this time. You should meet them alone."

"Okay, I'll ring him back."

She watched as Marcin went to have a shower.

They had a routine now. He'd run along the canal or the river come straight back to hers and have a shower before they'd either go out for dinner or cook together then watch TV. He'd walk home later.

She called her uncle and he made the arrangements there and then. She was to leave later in the week.

***

Sweden was glorious.

Meeting her aunt who was just a baby when her father, Alrick, had died, had been very emotional.

Fliss had lots of cousins and learned that the family was wealthy and generous with it.

She was now entitled to her father's estate, an estate worth a considerable sum of money. Fliss had tried to say no, but they were having none of it. Not only could she buy a house with her mother's money, she could buy several with her father's and if she was careful she'd even be able to travel for a year.

She'd also met the jilted bride, happily married to the man Alrick had helped her run off with.

Fliss was sat in the kitchen reading the Nottingham news online when she'd learned that Marcin had been in an accident on the ice.

He was in hospital with an injury that could threaten his whole career, it read.

Uncle Jorgen drove her to the airport and she took the next flight out. She got to Queen's Medical Centre later that afternoon.

It wasn't visiting time but, after explaining that she'd just flown into the country, the nurses allowed her ten minutes and showed her where his room was.

Fliss was about to enter when she saw them. A pretty, dark-haired girl was already there, sat on the edge of his bed with her head leaning against his shoulder. They were talking quietly and he was playing with her fingers.

It was obvious that she wasn't his sister by the intimacy of their embrace and, unseen, Fliss stepped back and, in a daze, went home.

CHAPTER THIRTY-THREE

Fliss took a taxi back to the hospital. It was very late, way past visiting hours, but she wanted to ensure that she didn't bump into anyone. Her.

The chances of her getting on the ward were slim to non existent, but who looks at someone in crutches in a hospital? She reasoned, making her way to his ward.

She couldn't believe her luck, the janitor had wedged open the door with his trolley and was busy in an adjacent room.

As quietly as she could Fliss, walked down the corridor. The nurses were talking in a back room so Fliss made her way as quickly as she could to his room.

He was alone.

She watched him for a moment before walking around his bed leaning on her crutches as she took in his injuries.

His face was battered black and blue and there was a cut across the bridge of his nose. There was also an alarming amount of white dressing on his right thigh.

"Marcin?" She whispered.

He opened his eyes and turned to her. She saw his confusion and then the guilt before he shielded his eyes and looked down.

"I'm sorry, I just heard."

"Felicity, what are you doing here?"

"I saw the accident online this morning. I flew straight back."

"Just now?"

She could hear the nervousness in his voice.

"It's okay Marcin," she soothed. "I saw her."

He looked at her then, his brown eyes a mixture of pain,

embarrassment and relief.

"I'm sorry."

"Always the truth yes?" She said, using his words.

"Always the truth Felicity."

She could tell he was upset. Marcin was a rare breed, noble, honest and kind.

"Sit down Felicity, you shouldn't be standing like that."

Fliss looked around for a chair and, leaning her crutches against the bed and balancing on one foot, she quietly pulled out a chair hoping not to wake the one other patient in the room or alert the nurses to her presence.

She took his hand and he curled his fingers around hers.

"I came by earlier, straight from the airport and she was here. That was Agnese right?"

Marcin nodded.

"She has been here since the accident," he explained cautiously. "Came straight away."

"I'm glad."

He looked at her, his eyes widening briefly.

"I'm glad you had someone with you." She kissed his bruised knuckles tenderly. "I care for you Marcin, very much. But she loves you."

A single tear trickled down her face.

"I saw it today," she went on passed the lump in her throat, "I saw the love the two of you have for each other and I don't want to get in the way of it."

"Felicity..."

"No, let me finish. I know you care for me and I thank you for being so special and so giving and so warm. I will always cherish the time we had together Marcin." Her tears were falling unchecked. "But I don't want you to make the same mistake I made."

He squeezed her fingers.

"Close your eyes," she instructed. "Go on close your eyes."

When he closed his eyes Fliss spoke again, remembering what Mrs. R had told her.

"When you're old and grey who do you see beside you? It's not me, it's Agnese and that's okay. I promise you that it's okay."

She watched as a tear fell from the corner of his eye into his hair. He urged her closer.

"You are a special lady Felicity and I will always remember you and our times."

"I love you Marcin." She choked. "Just not in that way."

"And I love you too Felicity." He laughed through his tears.

"You really are a gentle giant." She sniffed as she carefully hugged him and buried her head one last time in his neck to breath him in as he held her close. She'd miss the affectionate security of his embraces.

"What happened to you?" She finally asked, pulling away and wiping her eyes on the cuff of her jumper.

"There was a fight, a pile on and a little cut on my thigh." He listed.

"Prognosis?"

"Not as bad as the papers made out," he answered lightly, but frowned at her. "Where will you go? What will you do?"

She smiled, trying to pull herself together.

"I'm going to do that singing thing. Go back to Sweden and from there I'm going to see the world. Alone."

"If things were any different..."

She put her finger to his lips.

"Shh, don't," she whispered gently as she picked up her crutches. "I'll never forget you Marcin. *Uz redzesanos.*" Goodbye she spoke in his language.

"*Uz redzesanos* Felicity." He said quietly watching her leave.

Felicity's luck continued as she left the ward unseen and went home with a heavy cast on her leg, but somehow lighter on her feet.

CHAPTER THIRTY-FOUR

"How do I look?"

"Fantastic!," Mackenzie answered again.

"Are you sure? I think maybe we should have gone with the red dress."

"No, you look gorgeous. Classy and different, not over the top." He scooted a look over at another contestant wearing a gold lame' *ra-ra* skirt with black studded boots.

Fliss looked at herself one last time. She was wearing the cream bandage dress with gold accessories and low heels as her ankle was still a little shaky now that the cast was off. She looked classy.

"What if I forget the words?"

"You won't."

"But I might."

"Fliss, you've practised. You won't forget the words. You look amazing and you'll be great," he soothed.

Fliss looked around the backstage area nervously. It was crowded and in chaos. Other contestants were singing to themselves in the mirror, one was crying, another taking off her make-up for the third time, Fliss realised, and a young lad was being told off by his parents.

"Tell me the rules again?"

"You need the sound leveller to reach red. The more you sing, the more the audience will participate, the higher the noise level. That's what we want, noise level. That way it won't matter what the judges say, we won't need their vote. It's all about pleasing the audience," Mackenzie explained yet again.

"Oh no." Fliss felt her stomach cramp and she tried to breath through it. She couldn't do anything about her elbow throbbing though. At least not right now. She'd been scared to take any painkillers in case they messed with her voice.

The girl who had taken all her make-up off was called, she wasn't ready and looked panicky as she tried to argue with the stage manager. Now or never the stage manager told her, if his gestures were anything to go by. The girl ran out in tears.

Fliss watched as the stage manager said something in his earpiece and, catching her eye, waved her over.

She wasn't supposed to go on for another fifteen minutes.

"You're on Felicity."

"But..."

She felt a pair of hands on her back propelling her through the black curtains.

One foot in front of the other, one foot in front of the other. Stand at the x she chanted as she walked the longest walk of her life. Get to the x, get to the x.

"Hello," someone said to her.

The lights were so bright she wished she had sunglasses, she couldn't see a thing.

"What's your name?" Merill-Lynne, the country singer from America asked her. You didn't need to see her to know that world famous husky voice.

"Felicity. Felicity Pecora."

"And what will you be singing today?"

Fliss named the song.

"Brave choice. Not many people can match those notes. Are you ready?"

"No," there were sniggers from the audience. "But I'll do the best I can."

There was a smattering of applause.

"Come on Felicity!" Fliss heard someone shout. "You can do it!"

"You have a fan I see," Merill-Lynne turned her chair around and looked into the audience. "A single fan."

The was more clapping, but not much.

Get the audience on your side, she remembered her coaching from Mackenzie. She can do this. She'd done this. She got this, she encouraged herself.

"I think I have more than one fan there Merill-Lynne," she said confidently.

There was laughter from the audience.

"Do you now?"

Fliss moved away from the X and peered at the audience.

"Oh yeah," she sang.

The audience responded with cheers and clapped when her voice went higher.

"Are you ready?" She sang out to all the people she couldn't see but knew were there passed the shadow of the judges table. "Come on are you ready?" She sang again showcasing the strength of her voice.

They loved it and without being told, Fliss went straight into the song. It was a popular chart topper that a number of different artists with different styles had sung. Everyone would know at least one version of it she thought.

She hit the notes and the audience sang along, she danced and she got them involved. Fliss was enjoying herself, then came to a huge ending, her voice projecting out across the stage.

The crowd cheered and whistled, stood up and clapped. The music leveller to the side of the stage hovered between the yellow and the red markers.

"You want more?" She asked them.

"More more more more," they chanted.

"I'll give you more," she went into an another song, not as well known but one that would showcase her voice, a love song, a story of love being lost. Everyone could relate to it and even though she'd practised it a millions times, the words still affected her.

She came to an end and the audience was silent.

Oh God, she was supposed to get them on her side, not crying their eyes out she thought, glimpsing a group of girls who had moved to the stage, crying and handing out tissues.

"Well well well," Merill-Lynne drawled. "You have a voice there don't you Felicity?"

Fliss smiled and walked back to the x. She hadn't even realised she'd walked so far from it. She could hear a buzzing in her head and the pain in her elbow was radiating down to her wrist now.

"Tell us about you Felicity?" Another judge, the producer/songwriter asked.

"Me?" She was coming down from the high. She could hear sniffles. "Not much to tell really."

"Why that song?" He asked, sounding genuinely interested.

"My friends made me sing it," she said honestly. She looked down. "I didn't want to."

"Why not?"

"It's too close to me. It tears me up inside every time I sing it."

"You sound as though you've experienced something like it. Loved and lost?"

She sniffed, remembering Teddy and Marcin.

"Haven't we all?" She replied honesty. "This past year I've met the two most wonderful men and neither of them are here with me now. So yes I've loved and lost."

"You've had it rough?" The country singer asked.

"That's an understatement Merill-Lynne. Men, they're just so complicated." She answered without thinking, and the women in the audience cheered and clapped.

"I like you Felicity. Tell me this though honey." Merill-Lynne asked. "Why are you holding your elbow like that?"

Fliss gasped and looked down. She was holding her elbow. It was hurting. It had been hurting for the past week. She knew it was the stress of the upcoming auditions, and not sticking to her pain management programme.

She looked up, seeing the smugness on the country diva's face. She wanted her to fail.

"I have a condition," Fliss began, walking to the edge of the stage and looking at all six judges. "It's called sickle cell. In times of stress, like now, my oxygen levels drop and my blood cells start sticking together and can't get through my veins. It hurts like f..."

The crowd laughed as she'd almost said the 'F' word.

"Well I guess you won't be of much use to us then will you?" The country singer said, with a hint of triumph in her voice. "This is a stressful business."

The audience gasped.

What a bitch, Fliss thought.

"Are you actually telling me that because I have a blood disorder I shouldn't follow my dreams?" Fliss asked.

The audience oohed.

The smile on the other woman's face dropped for a second, but went back in place and Fliss could see her fluffing her big hair.

Caught out, Merill-Lynne said. "No, not at all."

"Then what are you saying? We all," Fliss looked above the judges table and swung her arm to the audience, "we are all normal people, working day to day. I worked in a call centre on the night shift. We all have our dreams. I'm not going to let one little blood disorder stop me from following mine," she said, watching wide-eyed as the entire arena roared and clapped.

"When I come off this stage," she began again when the noise had died down a bit, "I'm probably going to have to get myself to the nearest hospital," she went on, "where's the nearest hospital?" She asked them all.

They answered.

"Thank you. And then I'll probably have to be on morphine and oxygen and if things are really bad have a blood transfusion," she explained. "But that's okay, because I know today I did the very best I could. I know I sang my heart out and meant every word I sang. I know that I followed my dream."

The crowd roared. The loudness monitor zoomed passed the yellow marker and went straight to the red, sirens and lights rang out and the crowd clapped harder, shouting and stamping their feet.

When the noise died down, Merill-Lynne stood up and walked to the front of the table to lean on it. Fliss could see her clearly for the first time.

"Don't you know the rules Felicity?" She asked with a malicious glint. "You need to hit the marker whilst singing. That little speech doesn't count."

The crowd booed.

"I didn't make the rules," the country singer said, turning to the audience.

Fliss was about to leave the stage when she heard a voice, a single voice coming closer.

"Excuse me, excuse me." A lady in the shadows said. "You, young lady, have no manners."

There was a ripple of laughter.

Fliss put her hand up trying to see passed the glare.

"That was the best audition I've ever heard," the lady said, reaching the judges table.

The audience cheered in agreement.

"You?" She went on. "Can't you give an old lady a chair?"

"You can have mine." The silent judge at the end spoke for the first time.

Fliss could hear a shuffle as she strained to see what was going on.

"Phew, that's better, thank you," the voice said, "let her sing another song."

"That's against the rules," Merill-Lynne said.

"She sang that first song without anyone asking, she can sing another one."

"Sing sing sing sing," the audience chanted.

Fliss didn't know what to do, her arm was aching and she felt faint.

Then she heard those few words above the noise.

"The apple Felicity. Take a bite of your apple!"

She looked out in confusion. Mrs. Rossington was in hospital in Newcastle. She couldn't be here.

There was a tinkle of laughter. "Of course, you didn't think I'd let a little old heart attack stop me from supporting my friend now would you? Now sing, before this man here decides he likes me and takes me off to his hotel."

There was another ripple of laughter.

Fliss found the X and started again. She was a bit wobbly and stopped. The audience fell silent.

Her apple she thought, this was for her, her mother and Mrs. R. Come on, focus.

The words came, her voice flowed and she belted it out. The music monitor went up and up and, before she finished, it hit the red and the sirens started, the lights were flashing and the arrow still didn't go down long after she sang her last note.

The crowd went wild. It was a full five minutes later that the stage manager came out and told them that she'd broken the machine and that they would have to unplug it.

The crowd loved it.

"Well well well," the judge on the very end said. He was some kind of billionaire music mogul. "I think we have ourselves a winner."

The crowd went wild again.

"You don't need our vote," he drawled. "You won honey!"

The crowd went even wilder.

"I won?" She couldn't believe it.

"Felicity Pecora have you had the time of your life?" He asked, smiling at her and saying those iconic words.

She paused dramatically before answering. "Yes!"

The audience cheered.

"What's your wish?"

The crowd hushed. Her wish? At this point everyone wanted the record deal or to sing in front of The Queen or in Vegas. She just wanted one thing, or maybe two things.

"I want," she began then added cheekily. "Can I have two?"

The crowd laughed.

"Depends," music mogul man said indulgently.

Fliss walked to the edge of the stage and peered out.

"I want," she began, finding the steps and walking carefully down them. The audience were so close she could see row upon row of people smiling at her, giving her the thumbs up and smiling through their tears. She made her way to the judges table seeing her friend for the very first time.

"To hug Mrs. Rossington."

Fliss saw tiny little arms opening wide and she dropped the mike and went into them, hugging the little lady and holding on for dear life.

***

It was the next day. As predicted, Fliss was in hospital attached to a drip. Mrs. Rossington was on another floor.

"Well that went better than just winging it," Mackenzie said, grinning, as he came into the private room courtesy of the TV network. "How do you feel?"

"Great, better than great."

"Why didn't you tell me you were in pain?"

She looked at him from beneath her lashes. "I thought I could pull through it."

"Don't do that again." He hugged her.

"Where are the others?" The *others* being the rest on pod eight.

"At the hotel. You've got a bevy of fans at the hospital entrance. You're a star."

"I don't want to be Mack," she told him honestly.

"I know you don't. But as your manager, I must tell you that you've got one last interview to do for the show. A follow up piece as they know it couldn't have gotten any better than it had last night. You made international news. I bet you'll even be on that American entertainment show!"

Fliss felt the heat of embarrassment touch her cheeks.

"When is the interview?"

"In here later on today."

"Here?"

"Yep, human interest and all that. Do you know what to say?"

"I know what to say. Have you seen Mrs. Rossington?"

"She's being interviewed as we speak. They'll be bringing her

216

down to see you soon. Now get some rest. It's going to be an emotional day." He kissed her cheek.

Fliss closed her eyes.

***

"So that's it?" Addison Johal said at the end of the interview, unable to keep the amazement from her voice. "You're donating all the money to the Sickle Cell Foundation and the Drug User Institute?"

"Yes."

"You are an amazing young lady Felicity Pecora and let me get this right? You don't want the record deal being offered?"

"That's right. Being on stage singing in front of all of those people was something I needed to do for me. I was taking a bite of my apple."

"You keep saying that phrase, how did it come about?" The famous journalist asked.

And so the interview went on. Fliss was exhausted by the time they were finally winding up.

"And for your second wish?" Addison asked. "Look into that camera there."

Fliss turned to the camera and thought of him. "You know where to find me," she said.

"And that's it. Our exclusive interview by Felicity Pecora the young lady who broke the noise leveller last night. Thanks for joining us. Goodnight."

***

My Dearest Felicity,

How lovely was it to actually meet in person? You are such a courageous young lady, beautiful and talented. I'm so proud of you.

We did show them on that TV show didn't we, and all the hoopla afterwards, well I was in my element I felt like a star again.

Fancy the BBC finding archives of me dancing with the troops how wonderful was that.

You have injected me with new life Felicity, but we must remember I'm an old lady and for the first time in my life I'm actually feeing a little tired.

There will be a time when my e-mails will cease and I want you to be ready.

With my last little hiccup I fought to come back, my dearest Mr. Rossington was there waiting for me and I almost touched his hand, but I thought, no not yet. I need to hear you sing.

The next time Felicity I'm going to go. I'm ready.

I'm glad you've decided to go back to Sweden for a while. There's nothing to keep you in England now that you and the hockey player have broken up. If you're sorry then I'm sorry. But now you're free to do whatever you want.

Remember freedom is a privilege for some Felicity.

Your friend
Alive but sitting with the wallflowers.

CHAPTER THIRTY-FIVE

Fliss learned to drive in Jamaica. She spent four glorious months living in Spencer's house whilst Della's house next door was being remodelled. It was strange to think they used to be playmates.

She'd learned to snorkel in the Florida Keys and had *sashayed* along Miami Beach in designer sunglasses. She'd sung in a dark club in New Orleans and dipped her toes in the Atlantic, she'd even been invited to sing at a Russian Oligarch's wedding, but had declined. Life was good. She had choices.

Now she was in Portugal. The country that started her travel bug and which was still her favourite place.

She decided she was going to buy a place here as the temperature was nice and moderate and her sickle cell was barely an issue.

Walking along the beach, she used her phone and checked her e-mails. She still hadn't received one from Mrs. Rossington. It had been four days, the longest it had ever been. She hoped nothing had happened to her friend.

Fliss had gone to see her before leaving England and remembered her surprise as the estate the older woman used to refer to was actually a real life estate with a main house, a gate house and a lake. A real one.

They'd had a giggle over high tea when Fliss had told her what she'd thought.

Now an avid planner, Fliss was going to drive over to Spain and visit Eddy and TT as they'd been tantalised by the warmer climate too. She couldn't wait to see them both, and Clyde.

Fliss stooped down, took off the leather sandals she'd bought from a little boy in Guatemala and walked to the ocean. She dipped her toes in the cool water and took a picture to add to the others on her social media page.

Fliss and her travels was the name of it and all you saw was her feet getting wet in various oceans, lakes and rivers across the world. It was quite funny how popular her page was.

Taking another photo for good measure, she kicked out and played in the shallows. The beach was empty except for a family further along and someone walking their dog off it's lead.

She was sure she'd seen a sign that said dogs needed to be on their lead? Oh well, not her business she thought.

Sitting in the sand she pulled her long dress over her legs and hugged her knees, thinking how far she'd come. Nice clothes with an appreciation of quality. She was sitting on the beach in the late morning sun wearing a floaty, gypsy style dress in soft pink and cream roses that reached her ankles, yet showed off more leg than a mini skirt as she'd undone all but three of the buttons on the skirt. It made her feel feminine and naughty at the same time.

She was at peace and so contented. No money troubles, a new family that loved her and cousins who dropped in on her whenever they could. She smiled. Her male cousins were so protective of her the one time she'd danced with a man in a club in Vegas, one of her older cousins practically dragged her away. She'd only laughed at their high handedness when they weren't around. At the time it hadn't been funny.

The man and the dog were closer and if Fliss didn't know Clyde was in Spain she would have thought this dog was his twin.

Tucking her head into her knees, she closed her eyes and listened to the sounds. Every beach had a different sound and she liked to pretend she could her the wishes of the earth with each sweep of the shore. Delicate and faithful in it's pull.

"Eww get off!" She shouted, scrambling to her feet when the dog attacked her with it's tongue. "Go away you crazy mutt!" Fliss turned to glare at it's owner but he was at least forty metres away.

"Oi!" She shouted, "can't you read the signs! Dogs on their lead!"

She gestured to the bright yellow and black signs along the beach.

Grabbing the dog's collar in case it attacked the children playing, Fliss waited for the man to approach. He was taking his time, she noted, and was actually talking on his phone. Fliss played with the dog's ears the way she always did with Clyde.

The dog was practically groaning in ecstasy.

"Don't you know dogs are supposed to be on their lea..."

No it couldn't be, Teddy? She closed her eyes and opened them again and looked around. Yes, she was still on the beach in Portugal. Yes, the children were still playing by the shoreline and yes that really was Teddy not five feet from her. She felt the darkness creep up on her.

"Don't you dare!" He yelled at her.

"Dare what?" Fliss snapped, grappling through the fog to look at him.

"Faint. We've waited ages for you to get here and now you're going to faint."

Fliss drew in the salty air. She needed to clear her head.

"We?"

"Me and Clyde." Teddy walked closer. "You know you've probably hurt his feelings."

"Why?"

"Not recognising him. He had a bath this morning especially."

CHAPTER THIRTY-SIX

Fliss looked down at the dog she was still holding by the collar. "Clyde?" The dog turned his head to look at her, his pink tongue hanging out of the side of his mouth and his tail wagging ferociously. "Clyde!" Fliss sank to her knees and buried her head in his neck. "Oh I've missed you. What are you doing here? You gorgeous boy, hey, have you missed mummy?" She asked him, completely unaware of how crazy she looked and how crazy she sounded.

She only let the dog go when he struggled against her embrace. And she stood up, wiping the tears from her eyes with her fingers. She hadn't seen him in months.

"What are you doing here?" She finally asked Teddy.

His lips tipped up into a slight smile and Fliss watched fascinated as his blues eyes touched every bit of her, lingering on her legs before he spoke.

"Waiting for you."

"How did you know I was here?"

"Easily enough," was his simple reply.

"Would you like to expand on that?"

"I don't want to say the wrong thing," he admitted, swinging the lead around in one direction and then the other.

Teddy didn't seem to be in any rush to explain his presence in Portugal, she thought.

"Clyde needs to be on a lead," she prompted, but he didn't move. Just watched her intently.

"I know but I thought you might walk off so I let him run to you to keep you on the beach," he finished, "for me."

Fliss waited for him to explain. He looked gorgeous in light blue jeans, thin white cotton shirt that was unbuttoned and flip flops. He was deeply tanned as though he'd been on holiday for weeks and he looked, she tried to name it, relaxed.

"Why?"

"You told me to."

Fliss thought back to their last conversation all those months ago, not remembering anything of the sort. "I didn't."

He stepped forward, close enough for her to see his beard trying to come through. Close enough to see what he wanted her to see.

She stepped back but he followed her move and captured her hand to lace his fingers through hers.

"I was your second wish."

He was. Fliss had given him her heart via that news interview whilst she'd still been in hospital. He never came for her and she started her travels without him, avoiding those countries they were supposed to see together.

"I couldn't come for you straight away as I had, well," he paused and rubbed the back of his neck, "issues."

"And those issues have gone now have they?" Fliss asked, struggling to keep the scepticism from her voice.

"Oh yeah," he grinned, pulling her forward with a sharp tug and kissing her deeply. He didn't need to coax her mouth apart as she let him right in.

The kiss was long and deep and everything she remembered.

"No more issues," he finished, tenderly cupping her face in his large hands as he looked at her.

"I love you Felicity Pecora and I've missed you." He dipped his forehead to rest on hers.

"I missed you too."

"And the love bit?"

"That goes without saying." She smiled through the tears that had begun to fall during his kiss.

He pulled her even closer, moulding her body to his, reacquainting himself with every dip and curve of her figure.

"Remember you once said you didn't have any close friends?"

She nodded, not wanting to move from where her face was plastered to his chest.

"Look over there."

Teddy turned her around by the shoulders and pointed to a group of people watching them, laughing and clapping.

Mrs. Rossington was in a wheelchair, Eddy and TT on either side holding her hands. Her cousins and Uncle Jorgen, Della and Spencer and she even saw Mackenzie giving her the thumbs up.

"I don't understand?" She said in confusion.

Teddy reached into his back pocket, went down on one knee and in the sudden silence held the ring up to her.

"Anywhere you go I go. Please say yes."

Fliss looked down at him.

"No."

CHAPTER THIRTY-SEVEN

Fliss spun on her heels and walked over to her family and friends who were looking at her expectantly, she could feel the intensity of Teddy's glare on her back as she sent them a look of apology before walking on.

"She said no," he told the group flatly.

Fliss heard Mrs. Rossington say into the silence left behind by his statement. "Well you best go about changing her mind then hadn't you Teddy?"

Fliss, blinded by tears, walked on then screamed when she was grabbed from behind and hustled up into a fireman's hold.

"What the fuck!" She struggled and kicked out. "Put me down!" She yelled at him as his long legs swiftly ate up the pavement.

"That's my girl!" Teddy chuckled, patting her bottom. "Swear to your hearts content, I've missed your foul mouth."

Fliss let loose a string of swear words then sobered when he entered a building. She couldn't see much more than the floor, but it was nice floor, clean and sparkly. A door opened and Teddy said thanks to someone, went up some steps and then into another room.

Her world righted when he tipped her back over and down onto her feet.

"What the f—hell was that?"

He grinned at her.

"Would you like a drink?"

"No I would not like a bloody drink, I demand to know why I'm here." She looked around the room. She was in a flat, a very bare flat if the lack of furniture and dust motes floating about were anything to go by.

"Good. I don't want one either. Come here Felicity."

She looked at him. He wasn't even breathing hard, she noticed as she wrenched her gaze away from the strip of skin she could see through the gap of his shirt.

"The last time you told me that you tried to seduce me," she reminded him candidly, planting her hands on her hips.

"So I did." He smiled, tipped his head to the side and stepped closer.

She thought he was going to pass her and go into another room but instead he went behind her and plastered her body against his, her back to his chest. His large hands moved against her legs from the tops of her thighs to the indention of her small waist and back again.

She could feel his arousal through her dress and tried to stop her body from pushing into it.

"What are you doing?" She breathed through the tightness in her throat.

He didn't answer but moved her hair, which was longer now, away from her neck to sink his teeth into her delicate skin.

With all her might she stepped away and faced him.

His blues eyes were smouldering and darker. He looked like a man deeply aroused as he watched her. His look alone almost made her whimper with need.

"I learnt a knew phrase on my travels Teddy," she said conversationally, trying to bring some order to her breathing.

"Oh yeah," his voice was deeper, huskier and sexier.

"I learnt the 'try before you buy' phrase." She stepped closer. "In Jamaica I'd try a single guinep before buying the whole bunch."

"Is that a fact," he said. He had no idea what she was talking about. He had no idea what a guinep was, he only saw the invitation in her beautiful eyes. He moved in and this time she really did whimper when he caught hold of her as she tried to run.

Run to where, she didn't know. The look on his face, the flare of his nostrils and she knew she wasn't getting away.

He pulled her into his arms and spun her around again. Again her back was pressed to him and he walked her a few steps to the wall. She caught the image of a county estate in a gold frame. It looked out of place.

Again his hands went to her legs up and down and he kissed her neck, nipping on the tender skin just below her earlobe before swirling his tongue in the delicate shell of her ear.

She pressed her bottom into him, she couldn't help herself and he answered by pushing into her.

The simulation of sex was as erotic as the actual thing, she thought, doing it again and again until, using his hips, he anchored her in place against the wall.

She could feel the coolness of it seeping through her summery dress.

"Please," she didn't know what she was asking.

Teddy slid down her body, hugging her hips and caressing her bottom through the floaty fabric before moving down her legs and back up again, taking the fabric with him and she could feel the roughness of his jeans against her skin.

His breath was hot in her ear. She wanted to kiss him, but he kept her in place. One hand bunched in her dress the other massaging her bottom as though he were moulding dough.

He was strong and the pleasure of his caress was almost painful, she had never felt such a sensation. Too much was hitting her senses at once. The coolness of the wall against her breasts, the roughness of his large hands and the heat of his breath.

"Please," she whimpered, as his hand scooted up between her legs. She moved them apart, giving him better access as he smoothed her back and forth through the silk of her panties. "Please."

She turned around then, almost throwing him off balance as she grabbed his head and brought his mouth to hers.

The kiss was hot, demanding that he pay attention as she bit on his bottom lip then smoothed the little nip with her tongue. She'd hurt him.

He took over, consuming her with his mouth pushing her into the wall and lifting her leg to wrap around his hip.

With only her shoulders supporting her she lifted her other leg to grind herself into his arousal. He made a noise and some awkward movements as he tried to touch all of her at once.

Adjusting them both, he pulled down the sleeve of her dress and kissed the sweep of her shoulder, he did it again on the other side, until her arms were bounded by the fabric.

"Please Teddy," she begged, desperate for him. She wanted more.

He smiled, looked into her eyes and pinched her nipples though the fabric of her dress and bra.

Her back lifted off the wall and he did it again, moulding her breasts before pulling the dress down to pool at her feet.

He stepped back.

"Beautiful," he said, seeing the coffee coloured satin against her dark golden skin.

His look brought tears to her eyes. She had never felt so feminine and beautiful.

He saw her tears and kissed them away. "Don't cry Fliss. Please don't cry," he begged, whenever his mouth left hers to skim kisses over her body.

Lifting her up with his mouth still attached to hers, he walked a short distance down a dark hall, before placing her ever so gently onto the bed.

She watched as he pulled off his shirt.

His tattoo.

It was the sexiest most tantalising design she had ever seen and she whimpered, feeling the throb that was for him, between her legs. She pushed them together, all the while her eyes glued to his body as he undressed revealing more of himself.

He was beautiful. All hardness, smooth skin, muscle and ink.

She moved to the edge of the bed and touched him. Tracing the swirls of his tattoo with her tongue whilst reaching up to tweak his hard nipples.

His arousal nudged against her chest and she wrapped her fingers around him bringing him to her mouth.

He felt so good. He tasted so good. She'd missed him so much.

He pulled away from her, he didn't want this first time to be about him, this was about her. All her.

Leaning forward and opening her legs he stroked the inside of her thighs. She watched him through her lashes. His look was almost reverential as he moved in to sweep his tongue against her skin. She whimpered, her hips inviting him further and he nudged against her with his nose before burying his face to breath in her aroused scent.

"Please Teddy," she begged, feeling the tremors start. Her toes curled when he dragged her panties down her legs. Her legs fell apart when he sucked gently on her swollen lips before climbing up to stab at her belly button with his tongue and trace a wet path to her breasts.

Her bra came off and he spent several long minutes sucking her dusky nipples, one at a time, deep into his mouth.

Fliss was in tears. She was an aroused mess. Pulling at his hair, pulling at the cotton sheet beneath her until, finally, he moved up still further, captured her mouth and entered her at the same time.

Fliss lost her breath as he filled her up. She had never forgotten the way he felt, had relived this feeling many nights on her own, but the reality of his breadth, stretching her, filling her, was like nothing she remembered.

He gathered her closer, buried his face in her neck as she pulled him in, wrapping her legs high above his waist, to take more of him. She was his, taking everything he had.

Her orgasm ripped through her and she screamed, but still he pounded into her.

He moved his hands to her bottom and lifted her still further into him and lost control.

She felt every tremor of his body, she felt him burst and pulsate inside her. She felt his hot breath as he slowly lowered her to the mattress and gathered her close to kiss her neck tenderly.

***

It was several minutes later before either of them even stirred. He was the first to move. Turning onto his side and pulling her into him.

"Okay?" He asked as he stroked her chest and her breast with small brushes of his fingers.

"Hmm mm."

"Lost for words?"

"Hmm mm," she snuggled into him ready to fall asleep but her eyes popped open when he turned her roughly onto her back and leaned over her.

"Well?" He asked.

"Well what?"

"You tried," he said tersely. "Are you buying?"

His expression was so serious and Fliss, completely depleted, tried to comprehend what he was saying. Then she smiled and touched his brow tenderly as his blue gaze darkened.

"When the man I waited for has my name tattooed on his skin I think I'd better. He's mine," she said, using a finger to trace her name in the curls and swirls inked onto his side.

"You saw it?"

"Couldn't miss it. Come here." She ordered tenderly, already pulling him forward and opening her legs.

When they woke, the room was in darkness and Fliss could hear talking, lots of talking and music downstairs.

"Where is this place?" She asked, sitting up and smoothing her hair out of her face.

"A place I bought," he kissed her tenderly and sprang out of bed. "Come on, get dressed."

When he didn't hear any movement he turned to look at her and stopped.

She was so beautiful, all tousled and sleepy, her lips plump from all the kissing. She was looking at the ring on her finger.

"What's this?" She asked, arching a brow and holding her hand up to the light, turning it this way and that to catch the sparkle as it bounced around the room.

"Do you like it?"

He was nervous Fliss saw. It wasn't something she saw very often with him.

"Hmm, not..." she didn't finish as he dived on the bed and covered her mouth with his hand.

"Don't say it!" He warned, his blues eyes stormy with emotion. "I'll get you another one if you don't like."

"I love it almost as much as I love you."

He kissed her.

"I love you too." He looked over at the clock on the wall. "We'd better get up."

"Why?"

"Because our friends are waiting for us downstairs. It's our engagement party," he said, as though they were just going out to dinner.

"Pretty sure of me weren't you?" She swung her legs to the edge of the bed feeling the tenderness between her legs. "And how did you know where to find me?"

"Me and Mrs. Rossington are best mates." He threw her a wink. "Come on."

"Dressed in that?" She looked at the dress he was holding out to her.

"You'll look beautiful," he kissed her as he threaded her arms through her bra, clipped it in place, before pulling the dress over her head. "You can't put these back on." These being her underwear. He scooped them up. "Wet." He said with satisfied smugness and put them in his pocket with a sexy wink.

Fliss used his brush to brush her hair and his toothbrush to brush her teeth and then they walked downstairs.

"She said yes!" Teddy shouted to their friends when he opened the door.

The End

CAROLINE BELL FOSTER

About the Author

When I described myself to my friends I called myself an introvert and they laughed so hard I should really be offended.

I also consider myself to be very lucky as although born in Britain, I spent my formative years mostly in Kingston Jamaica with a long detour through Toronto and Nairobi. I married my college sweetheart David, have two amazing kids, a rabbit, and a cat. I've come full circle and live in Nottingham, just 12 miles from where I was born.

Since becoming a Mum I've also donned the 'headset' and worked in Customer Services firstly with an international flower company (being voted agent of the year worldwide) to working nights talking to overseas customers. Hence this series has been knocking around in my head for a number of years.

If you like this story and would like to read about another member on Pod Eight drop me an email.

Any feedback or review, good or bad would be greatly appreciated. Don't like the Britishness of this series? Just let me know, I don't bite (smile)

To keep up with me and my projects I'm on most of the social media platforms although active on some more than others.

Caroline. X

Facebook: Caroline Bell Foster
Twitter: @cbellfoster
Email: Caroline@carolinebellfoster.com
www.carolinebellfoster.com

More printed and e-books by Caroline Bell Foster

Ladies Jamaican written under Caroline Foster (LMH)
Caribbean Whisper's (LMH)
Saffron's Choice (LMH)
Call Me Royal (Sunshine Publications) - The Call Center Series
Book 1
The Cat Café (Sunshine Publications) - March 2015.

www.ingramcontent.com/pod-product-compliance
Lightning Source LLC
Chambersburg PA
CBHW061136170626
46809CB00003B/883